[DOUBLE DETECTIVES]

The Monkey Howled at Midnight

by Zack Norris

STERLING CHILDREN'S BOOKS
New York

For Philip and Dashiell

STERLING CHILDREN'S BOOKS

New York

An Imprint of Sterling Publishing
387 Park Avenue South
New York, NY 10016

STERLING CHILDREN'S BOOKS and the distinctive Sterling Children's
Books logo are trademarks of Sterling Publishing Co., Inc.

© 2011 by Dona Smith

ISBN 978-1-4027-7913-8

Library of Congress Cataloging-in-Publication Data
Norris, Zack.
The monkey howled at midnight / by Zack Norris.
    p. cm. -- (Double detectives)
Summary: When twins Otis and Cody Carson, their father Hayden, cousin
Rae Lee, and family friend Maxim go to the Amazon jungle of Brazil, they
uncover a smuggling ring trafficking in endangered animals.
ISBN 978-1-4027-7913-8
[1. Smuggling—Fiction. 2. Endangered species—Fiction. 3. Rain forest
animals—Fiction. 4. Twins—Fiction. 5. Brothers—Fiction. 6. Amazon River
Region—Fiction. 7. Mystery and detective stories.] I. Title.
PZ7.N7995Mo 2011
[Fic]—dc22
                                                              2010048187

Distributed in Canada by Sterling Publishing
⅔ Canadian Manda Group, 165 Dufferin Street
Toronto, Ontario, Canada M6K 3H6
Distributed in the United Kingdom by GMC Distribution Services
Castle Place, 166 High Street, Lewes, East Sussex, England BN7 1XU
Distributed in Australia by Capricorn Link (Australia) Pty. Ltd.
P.O. Box 704, Windsor, NSW 2756, Australia

For information about custom editions, special sales, and premium
and corporate purchases, please contact Sterling Special Sales
Department at 800-805-5489 or specialsales@sterlingpublishing.com.

Designed by Susan Gerber

Manufactured in Canada
Lot #:
2 4 6 8 10 9 7 5 3 1
07/11

www.sterlingpublishing.com/kids

[Chapter One]

The man known as "The Chameleon" smiled to himself. The nickname suited him perfectly. His moods changed as fast as a chameleon changes colors. He could go from friendly to nasty in seconds. He had a cold, cruel streak. That was why he was one of the most feared people in the business.

What was his business? Smuggling. He didn't care what was trafficked. Anything that could be marketed was fair game. He dealt in whatever was in demand. He was in business to make money.

The Chameleon had become the most wanted smuggler in the world—and the most mysterious. Everyone was looking for him, and no one knew where to find him. He kept his identity hidden behind disguises and computer firewalls. His operation stretched over every continent.

The Chameleon liked to wear clothing made

from exotic animals. Right now he was wearing shoes adorned with the heads of extinct golden toads. Beside him was a cane encircled with a preserved snake, and around his neck was a very live python. His feet rested on a rug made from the skin of a rare ocelot. His umbrellas rested in a stand made from an elephant foot.

His illegal business had made The Chameleon a rich man, but he wanted more. He was smiling to himself because he was going to get richer. His smile grew wider as he thought about all the money he would make.

He was expanding his operation into an entirely new area. It was high profit and low risk. When he got things up and running he could double his money. The only hitch was in getting everyone to cooperate. His smile vanished. Nobody had better cause any problems. He was not a man to be crossed.

[Chapter Two]

"The river looks like a giant snake twisting through a huge forest." Otis squinted his brown eyes against the glare of the sun as he looked out the window of the airplane.

"*Niagara, o roar again*," said his twin brother, Cody. He pushed a lock of his brown hair off his forehead. "That's not original, but I like it."

Otis wrinkled his freckled nose and looked at his brother. "Is that the best you could come up with? It spells the same backward and forward, so it's a palindrome, and it's about water. But we're looking at the Amazon, not Niagara Falls. I mean, as a palindrome it kind of *falls* short in quality. It's really *all wet*."

Cody groaned. "Ha ha—like those puns of yours are any better. Next time try a little harder."

"Amphisbaena," their cousin Rae Lee piped up from the row ahead. She pronounced it *AM-fiss-BEE-na*. "It's a different kind of palindrome."

"What?" Otis and Cody said together. Their father, Hayden Carson, and their all-around friend and helper Maxim Chatterton echoed the word. The multitalented Maxim had started out as their father's agent and gradually became part of the family.

Rae sat up straighter and tossed her short black hair. "It's a mythical snake with a head at both ends of its body. I found it when I was looking through the dictionary and I memorized it for the trip. I figured Cody would have a palindrome about something and Otis would have a pun, so . . ."

"The word isn't a palindrome, but the snake is. Cool," said Cody.

"Awesome," said Otis. The twins each turned to the window. They were all quiet for a while.

Everyone in the group had been looking forward to the trip for weeks—especially the three 12-year-olds. It was summer vacation and they couldn't wait to see the Amazon rain forest.

Enrico Estevez, a wealthy Brazilian coffee merchant, had invited them to stay at his home in Manaus, Brazil. It was a city in the heart of the Amazon.

Cousin Rae Lee had been asked along because she was so into everything about endangered animals.

Months ago she had seen a program about them on television. She started doing research on the subject just about every day. Lots of endangered species lived in the Amazon rain forest.

"Did I tell you that toucans are endangered?" Rae asked out of the blue.

"Only about a gazillion times," Cody replied. "Y'know, usually it's Otis who gets obsessed with a topic, but when it comes to endangered animals you're right there with him."

"You were pretty obsessed with that haunted pirate story when we went to Calavera Island," Otis retorted. "What you're really obsessed with, though, is *talking. Blah, blah, blah, blah.*" Otis chuckled.

"Cut it out, you two," said Rae. "What's wrong with being interested in endangered animals, anyway?"

"Nothing," Cody replied. "I've got to admit, you've got me hooked on the subject. I know lots of endangered animals live in the rain forest—but I'm into finding out about *all* of the rain-forest animals. I know that even if you *could* see them all, there are so many that it would take months."

"That's right," Otis agreed. "There are about two thousand species of birds and mammals."

Rae began rattling off a list of animals. "Brazilian

5

tapir, jaguar, pink dolphin, scarlet macaw, hyacinth macaw, toucan, three-toed sloth, golden lion tamarin, harpy eagle, manatee—they're all endangered rainforest animals. There are more, too, but those are the ones I remember."

"That's a lot," said Otis. He swallowed. "Hey, my ears are popping. How long before we touch down?"

Maxim checked his watch. "Oh, should be about ten minutes now."

Mr. Carson cleared his throat. "There will be a little extra surprise for you all," he said. "I know you are going to ask me why I didn't tell you before, but you would have been pestering me every day. All I'm going to tell you is that you'll soon find out."

"Oh, come on, tell us," Cody asked eagerly.

"See what I mean?" said Mr. Carson with a mysterious smile. "You'd have been saying that every day for months. I'm not telling you. Not a chance."

When they stepped off the plane at the Eduardo Gomes International Airport in Brazil, they all felt as though they had suddenly been wrapped in a thick, soggy blanket inside and out. It was like no weather they had ever felt before.

"The air smells different," said Otis.

"Tropical," said Rae.

"I hope you'll get to visit the rain forest soon," said Mr. Carson. "I probably won't be going along with you, though. I think I'll be busy painting for a while." Mr. Estevez had hired Mr. Carson to paint his portrait. Hayden Carson was one of the most famous painters in the world. Everyone loved his work. Usually Mr. Carson liked to travel the world painting animals and nature, but he made pictures of people sometimes, too.

Mr. Estevez had been looking for an artist to do his portrait. When he saw the picture Mr. Carson had done of Jamal Mason, the young movie star, he knew that he had found exactly the right painter. He contacted Maxim and made all the necessary arrangements.

As the Carsons, Rae, and Maxim collected their luggage they saw a tall young man, about eighteen years old, coming toward them with long, sure strides. His eyes matched his black hair, and he had the broad shoulders of an athlete. He reached them quickly and held out his hand to Mr. Carson.

"You must be Mr. Hayden Carson. I've seen pictures of you. I am Pino Estevez." The young man smiled.

"I've seen your paintings, too. My father has shown us a book of them. He even bought two paintings."

"Really?" Mr. Carson raised his eyebrows. "Which ones?"

"*Sunning Iguana* and *Skull Island Afternoon.*"

"The ones you did on Calavera Island, Dad," said Otis.

"I remember them very well," said Mr. Carson.

"So do I," said Maxim. "I remember what happened on Calavera Island very well, too. I don't want to have any mysteries on *this* trip."

The young man knitted his brows. "Mysteries? What kind of mysteries?"

"It's a long story," said Mr. Carson. "Let's not talk about it now." He looked at Maxim. "Let's just say that the mystery we got mixed up in on our last trip was enough to last a lifetime. We want to relax."

Pino took them to a shiny black Cadillac. "It's my dad's car," he explained. "One of them, anyway. You'll all enjoy the air conditioning."

As they drove, the twins and Rae took in the sights. Manaus was a very modern city, though there were some beautiful old buildings.

"We live near the Teatro Amazonas, the opera house. It was opened in 1896. That was when Manaus was the rubber capital of the world. It's coming up on your left."

Everyone turned to look at a beautiful pink building with white columns and a dome that glittered with dazzling blue tiles. It was surrounded by trees. A few seconds later the car turned into a driveway flanked by ornate metal gates. Pino pulled to a stop in front of a mansion that looked a lot like the pink opera house, only white.

Everyone piled out of the car. The door of the mansion was opened by a gray-haired gentleman wearing dark trousers, a white shirt, and a black vest. There was a tiny monkey perched on his shoulder.

"It's a pygmy marmoset!" Rae exclaimed. "Oh, he's so cute. He would fit in the palm of my hand."

The gray-haired man smiled. "Welcome to the Estevez home. I am Carlos Santos, head of the household staff. This little monkey is a *she* and her name is Anjo. It means *angel*."

He reached up and scratched the monkey's chin. "You're my little *querida*. My little *bonequinha*. My little sweetheart . . . my little doll. You know we speak Portuguese in Brazil, don't you?"

"Oh, yes, yes," Rae and the twins said at once. They watched as two maids and three other servants came hurrying toward them.

"Someone take their luggage to their rooms. Another one of you show the way to Mr. Estevez," Carlos instructed.

A tall, smiling man with white hair combed straight back from his forehead appeared. He was wearing a tailored gray suit and had a glittering diamond ring on the first finger of his right hand.

"No need for that, Carlos," he said. "Here I am. Welcome, Mr. Carson, family, and friend." He beamed. "Come into my home." He led the way.

They all exhaled a long *aahhh*. The great entrance hallway had French doors that opened onto a garden, which exploded with colorful flowers. On the ceiling was a painting of the Amazon rain forest with animals peering out from behind trees and vines. The floor was marble.

"I hope that you'll all be comfortable here," said Mr. Estevez. "There is a swimming pool a short walk down the path behind the house."

Cody, Otis, and Rae exchanged glances. This guy had a swimming pool in the middle of the city. Right in back of his house. Well, that was someone who could afford to fly an artist and his family from another continent because he wanted his picture painted.

"I know we'll all be very comfortable in your beautiful home," said Mr. Carson.

He was about to thank Mr. Estevez when the sound of a crash and breaking glass came from somewhere in the house.

[Chapter Three]

They all followed Mr. Estevez, who hurried into the living room. A vase was shattered in pieces all over the floor.

"I'm so sorry. It was an accident," said a young man who was dressed in a blue T-shirt and cut-off jeans.

The twins and Cousin Rae gaped at him open-mouthed. He had dark eyes and dark hair, just like Pino. In fact, he looked *exactly* like Pino.

"There's your surprise," said Mr. Carson. "We're staying with twins."

"I'm Luis Estevez," said the young man. He glanced at his brother. "We decided that it might be fun not to let you know we were twins right away."

"Wow," said Rae. "You guys are as much alike as Cody and Otis. I couldn't tell you apart if you weren't wearing different clothes."

"Their mother was the only one who could tell

them apart," said Mr. Estevez. He looked down at the broken glass on the rug. "I'll have the butler clean this up," he said. "Why don't you all go out into the garden for lunch?" He opened the French doors and walked away.

"I hope to talk with you about painting, Mr. Carson," Luis called after them. "I'm a great fan of your work. I—"

"Stop talking, change your clothes, and get down-stairs right away," Mr. Estevez said gruffly. There was something about the way he spoke that let them all know he was used to telling people what to do.

In the garden, a long table was set for lunch. The variety of plants was dazzling. Orchids bloomed on the trees and ruby-throated hummingbirds and butterflies flew among the flowers. Mr. Estevez joined them. "I hope that you'll enjoy a traditional Brazilian dish," said Mr. Estevez. "It's called *feijoada.*"

"I know what it is," Cody piped up. "I read about it. It's smoked meat and seasoned vegetables with manioc and fruit. Manioc is a root, and it can be used like potatoes or flour."

"That's right, Cody. I hope you will enjoy it. To drink we have some tropical fruit juices—guava or passion fruit."

"This sure beats airplane food," said Otis.

Mr. Estevez laughed. "After lunch we can take a little tour of the city museums."

"Can we go to the rain forest soon?" Cody blurted out. "I'm sure the museums are nice but we've been reading all about the rain forest."

"Oh, Cody, really," said Maxim reprovingly. "Mr. Estevez has made plans for us. Don't be rude."

"No, no, it's quite all right," said Mr. Estevez, smiling. "You can go with my sons. They're certified rain-forest guides. How about tomorrow?"

"Great!" Cody said, grinning broadly at Otis and Rae.

Pino turned to Luis. "I have some business to take care of tomorrow. I think you'd rather go anyway, wouldn't you?"

"Uh—sure," said Luis. "I can ask Aldo to go along with me. He'll be coming to the museums with us."

"Aldo is a fellow Pino and Luis met while they were training to be rain-forest guides," Mr. Estevez explained. "He's become quite a good friend."

"Such a good friend, Aldo," Luis muttered.

Mr. Estevez's cell phone chimed. He answered, and they saw his face become redder and redder as he listened. "I'm not selling you my land. I told you several times before," he said through clenched teeth. "I'm not letting you turn more of the rain forest into a cattle farm!"

He ended the call and shoved the phone into his pocket. "I own many acres in the Amazon rain forest," he explained. "I think the land should remain as it is. But someone is always after me to sell it, including my own family."

"I don't think it would be such a bad idea, Dad," said Luis. "We could use the money for—"

"Stop!" Mr. Estevez threw down his napkin. "I have enough money and I'm not selling land so that Pino can throw his life away. Usually he is the one bothering me about selling land. I don't need you starting in on me, too." He glared at Luis, then at Pino.

A hush fell over the table. The silverware clanged as everyone ate in silence.

"This lunch is delicious," said Maxim finally. "My compliments to the chef."

"I just remembered that I forgot to wash my hands," said Rae. "Can I go do it now?"

"Go right ahead." Mr. Estevez smiled at her.

She left the table and Mr. Estevez looked around at the others. "I'm sorry I lost my temper," he said, "but the idea of selling my land always annoys me. I have to fend off offers nearly every day. This cattle baron was practically threatening me."

He looked from Pino to Luis. "Someday the land will belong to you, along with the coffee business."

"The coffee business isn't for everyone," mumbled Luis.

"No more talk about land sale and business," said Mr. Estevez firmly. "We're going to entertain our guests."

Luis looked down at his plate but said nothing. Pino shifted in his chair and pushed his food around.

Maxim cleared his throat. "I don't think I'm up to a trek into the wilderness tomorrow. I'll be happy to see a part of it in one of the tourist parks."

"Really?" Mr. Estevez raised his brows. "How about you, Mr. Carson?"

Mr. Carson put down his fork. "I would love to go, but I hope that we can arrange something later. I'd like to get started on that portrait tomorrow, if you don't mind."

"Yes, yes," Mr. Estevez said eagerly. "We must plan how I should pose. I want the picture to capture my personality. Do you think I should pose in a suit, to show that I am a businessman? Should I be on a horse, perhaps? Or should I be on my boat? Or climbing a mountain, or something else that I am good at?"

Cody and Otis exchanged glances. This guy had quite an ego.

"I'm sure we'll figure it out," said Mr. Carson.

"Wonderful." Mr. Estevez beamed. "Now let's all freshen up after lunch and then hit the museums."

Otis, Cody, and Rae waited for the others in the great hallway. "I've got something to tell you guys," said Rae. She leaned toward them.

"After I washed my hands I walked back through the living room. I saw a cell phone lying on the floor. I thought it was mine and had dropped out of my pocket when we ran into the room. It never occurred to me that it might belong to someone else. I picked it up and checked the list of calls to see if anyone had phoned. I found country codes in there from all over the world. Sixty-five, eight hundred fifty-two, um . . . sixty-one . . ."

Rae glanced upward. "Sixty-five, that's the country code for Singapore . . . and eight hundred fifty-two, that's Hong Kong, and sixty-one, that's Australia."

"How do you know all this?" asked Cody.

Rae shrugged. "I just got interested one day when it was raining, so I looked them up."

Otis nodded his head. "That's Rae, all right," he said. "Random-knowledge queen."

"Come on, Rae," said Cody, shaking his head. "Did you really think that cell phone belonged to you, or were you just being nosy?" He knew that Rae had a way of letting her curiosity get the best of her at times.

"Well . . ." Rae reddened. Then she shrugged. "When we left the dining room I saw Luis pick up the phone and put it in his pocket," she whispered. "He looked really strange—pale and kind of scared."

"I wonder why Luis was getting those calls from everywhere. Friends?" Otis wondered aloud. "I noticed something else. Pino and Luis don't get along very well with their father. It seems like he pushes them around."

Cody opened his mouth to say something but was interrupted by the sound of a loud argument. It was coming from behind two heavy doors that led to a room off the hall. One of the voices belonged to a twin. The other belonged to Mr. Estevez.

"I don't want to hear about it anymore!" he thundered.

"But, Dad, it can't just go on and on and on."

18

"I'll bet Mr. Estevez is arguing with Luis about selling land again," said Rae. "Let's wait out front. We don't want them to open the doors and find us here listening."

"That's right," Otis agreed.

They went out on the sunny porch. There was a man sitting down on the steps. He stood up when he saw them.

"I'm Aldo," he said. "You must be the Carson twins and Cousin Rae."

Aldo was an extremely tall young man with a shaved head. Broad shoulders and muscles nearly popped through his shirt. He looked like he could knock down a brick wall without trying hard.

Cody spoke up. "I'm Cody Carson and this is my brother, Otis."

Aldo nodded, then smiled at Rae. "I've heard about all of you."

At that moment Carlos appeared on the porch. "Did you deposit the check I gave you for helping with the garden?" he asked Aldo.

"Yes, I did," Aldo answered with a nod. "I did it last week."

"What check? What for?" Mr. Estevez asked as he walked onto the porch.

"Oh—I asked Aldo to fetch some plants to add to

the garden," Carlos explained. "I didn't pay an excessive amount."

"Good," Mr. Estevez said shortly. "Some people think I'm made of money. By the way, Carlos—you mentioned a raise. I really don't think it's necessary."

Carlos's face was expressionless. "Of course, sir," he said.

Rae and the twins cast sideways glances at each other. It was embarrassing to hear Mr. Estevez talk about money with his employee. It should have been done in private. But they had already begun to realize that Mr. Estevez didn't treat anyone with kid gloves.

Luis appeared with Mr. Carson and Maxim. "Let's start the tour," he said.

They went from the Museu do Indio to the Museu do Homem do Norte. They saw pottery and woven goods and materials from the native tribes. All day long, Mr. Estevez's phone kept ringing. "I'm sorry, but I can never ignore a phone call," he said. "It could always be business, and it could always be important."

Pino took out his phone in the Museu do Homem do Norte. "I'm turning mine off," he said.

Mr. Estevez looked at him sternly. "You should take

the business more seriously. So should your brother. You'll be running it someday." Then his phone rang again.

"No, no, no—it can't be done," he said, shaking his head. "I can't give you another chance. You've had too many already." He hung up and sighed.

"That was a former employee," he said. "I hate to fire anyone. But he just wasn't doing the job. I suspected he might be stealing, too. He denied it and I couldn't prove anything." He shrugged. "Well, let's keep on looking."

"It's a wonderful museum," said Mr. Carson.

Rae and the twins agreed. They were learning a lot. But they hadn't learned how to tell the Estevez twins apart.

Moments later, Mr. Estevez got another phone call. As he spoke, his voice shook with rage. "I already told you everything I had to say," he snapped. "I am here with friends at the Museu do Homem do Norte and I would like to enjoy my day. I don't want to hear from you again. Ever." He hung up.

"Same disgruntled employee?" Maxim asked.

"Uh—yes, yes it was," he answered. He clenched his jaw tightly.

About half an hour later they left the museum

and headed out into the warm sunshine. "What would you all like to do?" Mr. Estevez asked. "We could visit our famous floating dock. It was specially made to rise and fall with the river water."

"That sounds really interesting," said Otis.

"It does," Cody echoed.

"I'd like to see it, too," said Rae.

"It sounds like a plan," Mr. Carson agreed. "Which way do we go?"

"Follow me," said Mr. Estevez. He stepped off the curb.

A black sports car came rocketing through the traffic, hurtling along at a dizzying speed. It swerved giddily along, dodging through traffic like a pony in a barrel race. Horns honked wildly.

There was no mistaking where the car was heading. It was streaking right toward Mr. Estevez!

[Chapter Four]

The Chameleon said good-bye and put down the phone. His eyes had turned from gray to black. He grabbed the snake that was hanging around his neck and flung it across the room. It hit the floor and began to curl itself up into a ball.

The man could smell a problem coming a mile away. He could sniff the stink of one in the air right now. This guy wasn't going to cave in.

He put in a call to his chief contact in Brazil. "Your friend isn't going to cooperate," he said. "I want the problem taken care of. This time, do it right."

[Chapter Five]

"Thank you, boys, for pulling me back just in time," Mr. Estevez said shakily. "You saved my life."

"Anybody get that license-plate number?" Otis asked. The car had sped around the corner so quickly that even his eagle eyes hadn't caught it. Everyone else shook their heads.

"There are some crazy drivers in this city," said Aldo.

"That didn't look like some random crazy driver," Rae observed. "It looked like he was trying to run down Mr. Estevez."

"The same thing happened last week, Dad," said Pino. "Remember when we came out of the bank?"

"Well, that car wasn't going as fast as this one," said Mr. Estevez. "It was just a coincidence." He took a couple of deep breaths. "There *are* some crazy drivers in this city."

"What about that disgruntled employee?" asked Otis. "Maybe he followed you. Or maybe it was someone else who knew you had gone into the museum."

"I think we should tell the police," said Pino.

"No! No police." Mr. Estevez waved his hand. "I don't think anyone is trying to kill me. My former employee is no murderer. Besides, he's in Rio de Janeiro, where most of his family lives. I know, because I paid for his plane ticket and saw him board. I drove him to the airport."

"Oh, come on," said Aldo. "It was just a crazy driver heading for an accident."

"It better have been an accident." Luis glared. He clenched his fists at his side. "Anyone who deliberately tried to hurt my father would have to tangle with me."

Later, back at the Estevez mansion, the twins and Rae took a walk in the garden. They wanted to talk over what had happened that afternoon.

"I'm not so sure it was an accident," Otis said. "That car was heading straight for Mr. Estevez."

"I still think that employee he fired could be the culprit," said Cody. "Maybe he wasn't in Rio de

Janeiro at all. Maybe he came back to take revenge on Mr. Estevez."

"Maybe he did," Rae agreed. "You know, I'm always telling you not to look for mysteries everywhere, but I have to admit that it looks like something is going on here."

"The numbers in Luis's phone may not be a clue after all," Cody said, shoving his hands in his pockets. "I noticed that Pino and Mr. Estevez had exactly the same model. Maybe they got them mixed up. If the phone I saw Luis pick up really belonged to Mr. Estevez, it's probably perfectly reasonable to have all those numbers since he does business all over the world."

He stroked his chin. "Actually, it might be reasonable if the phone belonged to Luis, also. Both brothers are in the coffee business."

"Maybe Mr. Estevez is mixed up in something shady," Rae said.

"Excuse me."

Rae and the twins jumped. It was Pino. He had crept up behind them so quietly they hadn't heard a thing.

"I couldn't help but overhear you talking about something going on. Nothing is going on here, I can assure you." He smiled a smile that didn't make it to his eyes. "My father isn't the kind of man to get *mixed up in something shady.* There is no need to worry him about a plot on his life. I don't want my father scared."

"We aren't going to do anything to scare your father," Cody said.

Then Pino smiled a real smile. "Good," he said. "I've heard that you three like mysteries. You've obviously gotten carried away. No harm done."

But before they turned in for the night, Cody, Rae, and Otis gathered in the twins' room and shut the door. "I don't care what Pino says. There *is* something going on here," Otis said in a hushed voice.

Outside the door, a floorboard creaked. There was the sound of footsteps hurrying away. Had someone been listening?

Moments later, they heard the voice of Mr. Estevez. He was talking to someone on the telephone, and he sounded very angry.

"Listen to me. I think you were responsible for what happened today. You aren't going to threaten me and you aren't going to scare me. I am not going to sell you that land in the rain forest."

[Chapter Six]

The next morning they all met in the garden to have breakfast before the trip. Rae and the twins could hardly wait.

"I can hardly believe our good luck," said Cody. "We're not just going to a park where the tourists go. We're going deep into the Amazon."

"Well, you're not going *that* deep." Luis chuckled. "That's where the tribes no one ever sees live. But you're going in deep enough. Can you please pass the fruit salad?"

Otis handed him the bowl. "I'm glad you're going with us," he said.

"Actually, Luis isn't going," Pino said.

Otis put down his fork. "What do you mean? How can we go if he's not going?" he cried.

Rae and Cody waited to hear the answer, forks suspended in midair. Did that mean they weren't going to the rain forest that day? Why were Luis and Pino grinning?

"Calm down," said Pino. "My brother will go with you."

Cody frowned. "I'm confused. What's going on?"

"I think it's time to tell them the truth," his brother said. "The two of us have been playing a little trick on you. You probably know the game. All twins do. We've been pretending to be each other. I'm Pino." He pointed to his brother. "And that is Luis."

"Yeah, we know the game," said Otis. "But we never caught on. How could we when we can't tell you apart?"

The real Pino shrugged. "We thought that as twins you might be able to see other twins the way most people can't. We wanted to see if you'd figure it out."

"Maybe they would have if they stayed around you for a while," said Rae. She put down her fork. "I can tell Otis and Cody apart, but most people can't. I've known them all my life."

"Well, we were just trying to provide a little fun," said the real Luis. "No more playing games."

"No more playing games," Pino agreed. "Let's finish up breakfast and get going. Aldo is coming along with us. We'll drive past the area of the tourist parks and fly upriver. Then we'll raft for a while and go inland."

"We'd better start packing," said Rae.

"Don't worry, we have everything you need," said Pino. "Just be sure to wear hiking boots, and bring some long pants and a long-sleeved shirt. The mosquitoes get really, really bad sometimes."

He turned to Mr. Carson. "Can they camp out for two nights?"

Mr. Carson nodded. "Yes. I've talked it over with Mr. Estevez. But be extra careful."

"We will. Let's get going," said Pino.

Even though Pino said that everything was taken care of, it didn't stop the twins from taking their own gear. They had always lived by the Boy Scout motto, "Be prepared." Their cousin was the same way.

Each of the twins packed a lightweight hammock and poncho in a backpack with mosquito netting. Each of them had their own compass, army knife, bottle of iodine pills (to purify water), extra pairs of socks, and sunscreen. They also packed bandages, plenty of mosquito repellent, matches and a magnifying glass, and a flashlight.

"Got all your stuff?" they asked when they met

Rae downstairs. She rattled off the same list of things that the twins had packed.

"I brought these, too," she said, holding up a pair of binoculars.

"Awesome, Rae," said Cody. Now they were ready to go.

"That's some trick they played on us," said Otis as they headed downstairs. "We haven't played that game in years. They are definitely too old for that." Cody shrugged. "I guess they figured we'd enjoy it." Otis wrinkled his nose. "Go figure."

They found Aldo sitting on the porch steps. When he saw them he didn't say a word; he just looked up and nodded. A few moments later, Pino appeared. He was carrying a camera with a telephoto lens strapped to his shoulder.

"You're a photographer? Cool," Cody said.

Pino nodded.

"Shouldn't you turn the camera around?" Rae asked.

Pino looked at her blankly.

"If you carry it like that, the lens is more likely to hit something than if it's facing backward," she explained.

Pino blinked. "Oh—of course. I don't know how

I forgot," he said, turning the camera around. "I guess I've got a lot on my mind."

They drove for hours, past the lines of people waiting to get into the nature parks. They had gone from a highway to a smaller paved road and then turned onto a dirt road that ran beside the Amazon River. Aldo pulled the truck off the road and parked behind some trees. "Here we are. The second part of our journey is ahead." He pointed to a plane that sat on an airstrip among the trees.

"You're not afraid to fly in a small plane, are you?" Pino asked the twins and Rae.

"Absolutely not," Cody answered, adjusting the backpack on his shoulders.

"No way," said Otis.

"Nope," said Rae.

Pino looked at the three of them. "Then let's go," he said.

[Chapter Seven]

They were landing on an airstrip behind a village on the bank of the Amazon River. "People here have a foot in two worlds. Let me explain what I mean," said Pino. "They still hunt and fish and grow their own food. They know old customs and old ways. But they know all about television and radios and computers and cars and stuff, too. They also dress in modern clothes."

"When can we see the native tribes that are just the way they've been for centuries?" asked Rae.

Aldo started to laugh. It wasn't a funny laugh, either. He was laughing at Rae.

"Do you think those tribes are on the lookout to welcome us? They don't want to be found," he said. "They moved away from civilization, far into the forest. If you were standing next to one and he didn't want you to see him, you wouldn't."

"You'd have to go far into the jungle to see tribes that are untouched by civilization," Pino said. He didn't laugh. "There are hardly any—at least, that we know about."

"Why are we stopping here?" asked Rae. She was glaring at the back of Aldo's head. "Why is there an airstrip near this small village when you can reach it by water? You must have had to remove hundreds of trees to make an airstrip." Her mouth puckered with disgust.

"Actually, we had to remove a thousand trees to make the airstrip," said Aldo. "We had to remove the stumps, too, or they'd just grow back. It wasn't easy."

The twins didn't like the smirk in his voice. But their minds were on another matter. Why had they taken so much trouble to build an airstrip behind this village? It was just a collection of houses on stilts and a vegetable garden. It didn't make much sense.

As the plane touched down, the villagers ran toward it. When they all got out, two men came through the crowd and began talking to Aldo and Pino in Portuguese. Pino said something to them and one of the men spoke to a third while gesturing toward the twins and Rae.

"We have to talk to these two men for a while," said Pino. "Then I'm going to take some landscape photographs. You can go with Tomayo and have something to eat. He speaks English."

"We aren't hungry," said Rae. "We ate right before we left."

"Then have something to drink," said Aldo. Annoyance flickered across his face before he and Pino walked away.

"What do you have to talk about?" Rae asked.

Aldo stopped in his tracks and turned around. From the look on his face it seemed that he might smack Rae right then and there. "Mind your own business," he snapped. They all wondered why he had gotten so nasty.

"Aldo, don't be like that," said Pino. He smiled at Rae. "You wouldn't be interested in what Aldo is going to talk about. It's boring." He turned to go.

"You forgot your tripod," Otis yelled.

"I won't need it today," Pino called over his shoulder.

Cody and Otis exchanged glances. They both shrugged.

Minutes later, sitting outside Tomayo's home and drinking guava juice, Cody asked for details. "Do Pino and his friend come here often?"

Tomayo laughed. "Those two aren't friends. They are business partners."

"What kind of business are they in?"

"The photography business," said a voice behind them. Aldo had returned.

"I almost forgot," he said. "I'm thirsty." He took a cup from Tomayo's hand and took a drink. "Don't bore these kids with talk about our business," he said, staring hard at Tomayo.

He returned the cup. "Well, I have to go take some photographs with Pino," he said. Then he was gone again.

"What do you mean they are business partners?" Cody asked Tomayo.

Tomayo fidgeted, looked down, and said, "They sell their photographs. The two people from the village help them find things to take pictures of."

Cody and Otis looked at each other. Otis had a book called *How to Spot a Liar Every Time*. They didn't need that book to know Tomayo was lying. But why?

After about fifteen minutes, Aldo and Pino returned. Aldo looked pleased but Pino didn't.

"Take many pictures?" asked Otis.

"Oh yeah, yeah, I did," he answered. "I was clicking away. I must have taken about thirty shots."

"Time to fly," said Aldo. "We've got more pictures to take."

Soon they were in the air again, only to land at another village. One thousand more trees and stumps had been removed. This village was almost exactly the same as the last one. Except in this village, no one spoke any English. What was the need for another airstrip? There was no juice served this time. Otherwise, what took place was about the same as in the last village. Pino and Aldo left to talk to some men for about fifteen minutes. When they returned, neither one looked happy. They didn't say anything as they told Rae and the twins to get into the plane.

Cody watched Aldo and Pino carefully as they walked to the plane. Aldo's jaw was clenched. Pino's face was red. It looked like the two of them had been arguing . . . probably with each other.

He wondered if it had something to do with a small crate he'd seen being unloaded in the village. He'd watched as some men opened it and pulled out pistols. Why would they need pistols? Surely they didn't need them to hunt for food.

Cody followed Pino and Aldo as closely as he dared. He managed to catch some snippets of conversation.

"I can't believe they didn't find anything for us," Aldo said angrily. "Why weren't you tougher on them?"

"Because I'm getting a little tired of this whole thing," Pino said irritably.

"Well, get over it," Aldo snapped.

They hadn't said anything about guns. Cody's heart was hammering as he boarded the plane. He wanted to tell Otis what he had seen, but he couldn't while Pino and Aldo were around.

The rest of the ride down the river was tense. After a couple more hours, Aldo landed the plane on yet another air strip hidden among the trees.

Aldo insisted they get far away from the river. They walked for four hours before he announced that they could make camp.

The sunset was a beautiful pink and gold that cast glittering diamonds of light across the river. Birds soared into the treetops and sang out good night together.

Soon they were joined by other not-so-welcome companions. Swarms of flies and mosquitoes began to thicken.

They all sprayed themselves with insect repellent and put on long-sleeved shirts and pants. They stuffed the pant legs into their socks and sprayed some more. Scores of tiny black flies added themselves to the cloud of mosquitoes.

Aldo began hanging up hammocks and mosquito netting.

"I'm going to go get some firewood," said Pino. The twins and Rae insisted on going with him. At least moving around would keep some of the mosquitoes and flies away.

"Try to find sticks and branches that feel dry," said Pino. "It isn't so easy to build a fire in the rain forest because of the moisture in the air."

He was right. Even though everyone picked the driest wood they could find, it still took three tries to flame the fire.

From the cooler Aldo took fish wrapped in leaves, cheese, fresh fruit, bottled water, and juice. Rae and the twins heard their stomachs growling. They hadn't realized how hungry they were until they smelled the food cooking. When it was finally served they wolfed it down without a word.

"Oh, that was so good," Rae said finally. She wiped her mouth.

"Um-hmm," echoed Cody and Otis, who were still eating as fast as they could.

Aldo looked at them with a steely gaze. "I hope you three can do as you're told," he said in an icy voice. Pino looked at him and furrowed his brow.

Aldo stared back at him. "Don't give me that look. I mean what I'm saying." He got up and walked away.

"Don't worry about Aldo," said Pino quietly. "He just gets . . . nervous sometimes."

"Um, sure, we understand," said Rae. Cody and Otis nodded. The three exchanged glances. They all wondered about Aldo's personality change. Ever since the trip had begun they'd caught him staring at them from time to time with a stony expression. Otis wiped his mouth and yawned. "I can't believe how tired I am," he said. "I'm going to turn in."

"Me, too," said Rae.

They never went to sleep before nine, but the day had been so long and hot it felt like nearly midnight. Even Aldo didn't stay up much longer. Soon, just Cody and Pino were left sitting by the fire.

"I don't take many landscape photos," said Cody. "What f-stop do you use?"

"Two point eight," he said. "It's what I always use."

"Ah." Cody nodded. "I'll remember that."

The two sat in silence for several moments. Cody was about to turn in when Pino spoke up.

"I like your father," he said. "He doesn't bully you or your brother."

"You think your father bullies you?" Cody asked.

Pino poked the fire with a stick. "In some ways.

Like the way he says that my brother and I have to go into the coffee business. I want to go to art school and become a painter, but my father doesn't like the idea. He hasn't even looked at any of my paintings in years. I've asked him, but he refuses. If my mother were alive, maybe she could change his mind."

"A painter," Cody repeated, turning the idea over in his mind. It was a surprise. "What happened to your mother?" he asked.

"When I was eleven years old, she was flying back from visiting my aunt in Rio de Janeiro. The plane crashed."

Pino sighed. "My mother was the only one who could always tell my brother and me apart."

"You must miss her," Cody said quietly. "My mother died in a car accident when Otis and I were babies. I don't remember anything about her really. Sometimes when I wake up I think I dreamed about her, though. My brother says the same thing."

"I still dream about my mother sometimes, too," Pino said, poking the fire again. After a few moments he yawned and stretched. "I'm getting tired," he said. "I guess it's the heat and all the traveling. You should turn in, too. We'll get an early start."

Pino got up and started toward his hammock. "Douse the fire before you go to sleep," he said and pointed to a bucket of water. "If Aldo and I are gone when you wake up, we're just getting more firewood. Don't go anywhere, okay?"

"Why don't you wake us up so we can help?" asked Cody, but Pino didn't answer. He just got into his hammock and pulled the mosquito netting over his head.

Cody sloshed water on the fire and turned in. He listened to the chattering of the tree frogs as he drifted off to sleep.

Hours later, he was awakened by a deafening, long roar. *Mooaaahhh!* He sat bolt upright. It almost sounded like a dying cow. *Mooaaahhh!*

Cody shook his head to get the sleep cobwebs out of his brain. Otis and Rae were awake, too. "What was that awful noise?" he asked.

"A howler monkey," said Rae. "They're considered the loudest land animal in the world."

"Louder than an elephant, even?"

"Louder than an elephant," she answered.

The howler monkey sounded off one more time. Cody and Otis believed that Rae was right. It was *loud*.

Rae switched on her flashlight. "Hey, guys?" she called. "I think Aldo and Pino went somewhere. We're all alone."

[Chapter Eight]

Cody and Otis switched on their flashlights. Aldo's hammock was empty. So was Pino's.

"Check the ground for snakes before you get out of your hammock," said Cody.

"Yeah, and check before you put your shoes on, too," said Rae. "I read about people finding snakes and bugs in their shoes."

In less than a minute they all had on their hiking boots and were standing near the dead fire. "Why would they take off like this?" Rae said.

"Who knows? It doesn't seem too good," said Cody. "It looks like they were in a hurry to get somewhere. They weren't too careful when they left. Look at the rumpled sleeping bags, and somebody stepped on a dish and broke it."

"I don't think the business that Pino and Aldo are involved in is photography," said Otis.

"Me, neither," said Rae. "I started wondering as soon as I had to tell Pino to turn his camera around. No photographer who knows what they're doing carries a camera on their shoulder with the lens forward. It could bang into things before you noticed they were there."

Otis nodded. "Yeah. At first I thought it was just a slip. He said he had a lot on his mind. But there were more things."

"Like taking landscape photos without a tripod," said Rae.

"That's right. The shots would all be blurry." Otis swatted at a mosquito on his arm. "He said he had taken thirty shots outside one of those villages. He wasn't taking sports photos. Landscape photographers take time to set up the shot. And then tonight he told me that he *always* sets his f-stop at two point eight."

"It's dead wrong," Cody said as he shoved his hands into his pockets. "He should have used, like, f-twenty-two. He's not into landscape photography, that's for sure."

He exhaled a long sigh. "Pino told me he wants to study painting . . . not photography. And his father won't pay for him to go to art school, so he needs to make money. I don't want to jump to any conclusions," he said. "But whatever he and Aldo are up to . . . well . . . I don't think it's any good. There is something I've been wanting to tell you both."

Cody crossed his arms. "At the last village, I saw some men unloading a crate. It looked like it was full of . . . pistols."

"Pistols!" Otis and Rae exclaimed together.

"Yeah. It doesn't make any sense, does it? The villagers wouldn't use pistols for hunting. The crate was small, so it wasn't like they were transporting mass quantities to sell. I just don't get it."

"Well, it doesn't sound good at all," said Otis.

"Maybe we should get out of here right now," said Cody.

The three looked at each other. "Nah," said Otis. "We need them to help us find our way out of this jungle. Let's follow them and see where they went. I want to find out what's going on."

"So do I," Rae said. "They took a lot of trouble to make those airstrips. It must have cost a lot of money. Too much money and trouble to spend a few minutes taking photographs."

"If he took photos at all." Cody sighed. "Okay, we'll track those guys. How far could they have gone?

I'll bet they keep the plane here because it's a place they come to a lot. Maybe there is something hidden around here."

"Let's make sure we can find our way back, though," Rae said.

"I'll mark the trees with my Swiss Army knife," said Cody. "We'll have to stick together. Nobody comes back without the other two."

"Unless one of us gets captured," said Otis.

"Or two get captured," said Rae.

"Let's just make sure that doesn't happen," Cody told them. "If they've gone too far, we'll have to come back to camp. We can't risk being caught out in the jungle overnight. We've got enough problems without that."

"Actually, Cody, we have more problems than you think," Rae whispered. The twins couldn't see her face in the darkness, but it had gone pale.

Something about the tone of Rae's voice sent a chill running up their spines. They turned slowly and saw two red eyes looking at them from the ground about six feet away. By the light from their flashlights, they could make out the form of an animal. It was a caiman—a crocodile. A big one.

[Chapter Nine]

Nobody moved. Nobody said a word. Nobody even breathed.

The three knew that if the crocodile took off, whoever he came for didn't have a chance. The thing to do if you see a crocodile is run—usually. If you are in reasonably good shape you could outrun it. That is because crocodiles are fast, but they tire quickly on land.

But this crocodile was so close, there was no way they could outrun it. They just had to hope it wasn't hungry.

Seconds ticked by. Each one felt like hours. Rivers of sweat ran down every forehead. Mosquitoes feasted and flies landed on faces and hands without being noticed.

"I hope you're working your animal magic, dude," whispered Cody.

Otis had a way with animals. Cody and Rae had seen him charm angry dogs. But he wasn't charming this crocodile.

The caiman took a slow, lumbering step forward. Then another. And then . . .

Splash!

An animal had just fallen into the river. What was it?

The crocodile whirled around so fast that its body was a blur in front of their eyes. There was another splash as it headed into the water. They heard thrashing for a few seconds, and then all was calm.

Still, nobody said anything. They all knew that something had been a meal for the croc. An unfortunate *something* that had saved them.

"I think I may be sick," Cody said finally.

"Me, too," said Otis.

"And me," said Rae.

"After that, what else can possibly scare us tonight?" Cody asked.

"Plenty of things," Otis replied.

"Yeah," Rae agreed. "Lots of things."

"Like a hungry jaguar or an eight-foot-long snake . . . or Aldo," said Otis.

"Well, then, we'll have to be really careful," said Cody. "Let's get going."

"Hang on," said Otis. "Cody, have you got those iodine pills in your backpack? Better bring them in case our canteens run dry and we need to purify some water. And don't forget the insect spray, and some allergy medication."

They all got busy finding stuff they thought they might need. Then they headed out into the jungle, using their flashlights to follow the prints of Pino's and Aldo's hiking boots. Right before she left, Rae tucked a camera she'd brought along into her pocket.

When they had been walking for about forty-five minutes, they began to realize that the jungle wasn't as dark as before—in fact, it was getting brighter and brighter. It wasn't the moonlight. It barely penetrated the thick canopy of trees. The light was coming from somewhere up ahead.

About ten minutes later, the trees stopped abruptly. Rae and the twins found themselves looking ahead to a clearing. What was in it took their breath away.

Surrounded by a chain-link fence was a huge one-story brick building that looked like a giant warehouse. There was a guard with a rifle on patrol at the open gate.

"Let's see if there are more guards," Otis whispered. "This is a big place for just one of them."

Sure enough, about a minute later a second, taller

guard rounded the corner. In another minute, they watched the first guard pass by again. They waited a few more minutes to see if there were any more. There weren't.

"It looks like there are only two," Rae said softly. "We have a minute to get through, but we can't make any noise."

"Start moving after the first one rounds the corner," said Otis.

Cody and Rae nodded. The moment the first guard passed, they got ready. Then they started to move.

Before they had gotten clear of their cover, they heard a bone-chilling roar. Another one, even louder, followed. They froze in their tracks as one of the most beautiful animals they had ever seen streaked past them in a blur of gold and black.

"Jaguar," Otis breathed in a whisper.

The animal raced toward the fence and launched into the air. Animals inside the compound were already chattering, warning of danger. The yard erupted into a frenzy of activity. At least ten guards showed up, all jabbering at once.

As the jaguar flung itself over the fence, one of the guards took out a pistol and fired. Cody, Otis, and Rae

each stifled a desperate cry as they saw the animal claw
at the air and then fall to the ground.

The guards gathered around the jaguar. "He'll be
all right," they heard one say. "Get him back to his
cage. How'd he get out?"

"Tranquilizer guns," Cody whispered. "That's what
I saw them unloading from the crate in the village."

Otis nodded. "Let's move."

They hurried past the distracted guards through
the gate and toward the building. Otis pointed to
a surveillance camera just over the door. They all
crouched down low and prayed that it didn't pick
them up. Then Otis reached up and opened the door.

He pointed one finger under each eye, and then
pointed upward. Rae and Cody nodded to show that
they knew what he meant. They had to keep an eye
out for more cameras.

They found themselves in a long hallway with
rooms leading from either side. Hearts hammering,
they walked past an office. There was a computer on
the desk with images of the different rooms.

"Nobody's checking the cameras for now," Cody
whispered. "But we should still try to keep away
from them."

Otis and Rae walked ahead. Cody glanced into

the office and saw an open drawer underneath the computer. An official-looking document inside the drawer caught his eye—it was signed very clearly "Enrico Estevez." Then he saw the words "Bill of Sale." Almost without thinking he reached out, grabbed the sheet of paper, and stuffed it into his back pocket. Then he walked after the others. He would share with them what he had found when they were somewhere safe again.

They entered the second room. It was huge, with rows and rows of stalls that had partitions about three feet high. Cody and Otis peered over the side and found that some held medium-sized lizards and tortoises.

They walked to the end of a row of stalls and found three heavy doors with thick glass windows. Through them they could see thermostats on the walls. They were temperature controlled. This was a big, professionally run business.

Behind one door were brightly colored frogs; behind another were beautiful birds. Rae recognized rare blue hyacinth parrots. Behind the third door, in a large tank, a lone animal swam listlessly. It was a rare pink river dolphin. Rae's heart plummeted. She knew those animals were sometimes killed for their eyes and teeth. Some people thought they were magical and used them to make charms.

Suddenly some monkeys began chattering and jumping all at once. Some of them hurled themselves against the chain link walls of their cages. Above the animal noises they heard human voices calling loudly to each other in Portuguese.

Workers would soon come to see what had caused all the fuss. If Rae and the twins didn't get out of there fast, they'd be found for sure.

Cody held a finger to his lips and hissed, "*Shhh!*"

Rae and Otis both nodded with exasperation. Did he really think he needed to tell them to be quiet?

Since Cody was nearest to the door, he moved quickly to hide behind a row of cages and waved the others to follow him. Otis lifted his feet carefully, trying to make as little noise as possible with his hiking boots. Rae hurriedly clicked a couple of pictures and then caught up with him. They had just reached the area behind a stall where turtles were kept when they heard footsteps outside—running.

Cody silently motioned to the others. They backtracked their steps and edged into the office. Then they waited, hearts pounding.

The men raced toward the monkey cages. They

checked one after another, talking in excited tones. Then Rae and the twins heard the footsteps of two more men. These two weren't running, but their steps sounded firm and sure.

"These dummies think the monkeys might be sick." It was Aldo's voice. He was talking to Pino in English so that the others wouldn't know what he was saying about them.

"It's not such a stupid idea, really." That was Pino's voice. "These monkeys shouldn't really be caged up inside. Maybe it *could* make them sick."

"Maybe you thought that jaguar was sick, eh?" Aldo asked accusingly. "I hope you weren't dumb enough to let him out of his cage."

"What's dumb is keeping these animals caged up. It's beyond dumb; it's cruel," Pino replied.

"There's something wrong with you." Aldo's voice was full of contempt. "They are just animals. Animals that will bring us a lot of money. Are you forgetting that?"

"I'm not forgetting anything." Pino's voice was angry. "I'm just not sure it's a good idea. Waldo Lou is trapping too many animals to be killed. Tigers are chopped up and eaten by people who think tiger meat will make them strong. Lizards are ground up to make medicines that don't even work. Elephants are killed for ivory. Lots of the animals he gets are endangered. I don't think I like working for someone like that."

Aldo laughed. It wasn't a funny laugh, but a nasty one.

"These animals aren't going to be killed—except maybe the turtles. Lots of people think turtle meat is mighty tasty. These animals are going to zoos and aquariums, and to be exotic pets. People pay big money for one of these little gold monkeys, or the blue macaws—or one of those anacondas."

"Oh, come on, now. You know that the guy we work for kills animals. Maybe not these, but others. Rhinos for horns. Gorillas for paws. We can make lots of money. But it's wrong."

"What are you, a Boy Scout now? You didn't think it was a bad idea before. All you wanted was money to go to some fancy art school your rich daddy won't pay for. He wants to hand you a multimillion-dollar coffee business. Boo-hoo, he's so mean."

"I don't want to run a coffee business."

"Well, you're a lousy photographer. You barely know enough to take the lens cap off."

"You know as well as I do that the photography angle was just a cover for what we're really doing. I'm a painter, not a photographer."

"Oh? You think you're going to be another Hayden Carson?" Aldo snorted. "Let me tell you something, rich boy. You're going to play along. If you do anything to mess up this business, I'll tell your daddy what you've been doing. He won't like that. Meanwhile, get him to sell me this land."

"You wouldn't dare tell my father," Pino said. It sounded more like he was asking a question.

"Yes, I would." Aldo paused. "Maybe I deserve a little reward for not telling him about it. You could give me some money. I'll let you know how much."

"That's blackmail!"

"Bingo. You win. But if you tell anybody what is going on here, I warn you, you'll be in for a lot worse. You don't know who you're dealing with. The guy we work for doesn't play around. He's not just dangerous . . . he's deadly."

"Let's just make sure the monkeys are all right," said Pino after a moment. Cody and the others heard his footsteps as he moved from one cage to another, followed by the heavier trudging of Aldo's feet.

"Looks like everything is fine," Pino said finally.

"I told you so," said Aldo. "Let's finish getting the packing crates ready for shipment. We'll put some of those little lizards that jump and bite on top of the snakes. Inspectors get sick of being bitten and move the crates along."

"Okay, okay. But we've got to get back to the kids at the camp."

"Aw, don't worry about them. The little geniuses will be just fine. It might do them a little good to get scared, anyhow. They think they know everything."

Cody, Otis, and Rae stood perfectly still as Pino and Aldo left with the workers and turned off the lights inside the warehouse. They could still see the lights from the yard outside streaming through the windows.

"So we were right about Pino. He's involved with an endangered-animal smuggler," Rae said with disgust.

"Hold on now," said Cody. "It sounds like Pino is having serious second thoughts."

"Yeah, but it doesn't sound like Aldo's conscience is bothering him," Otis observed.

"True," Cody agreed. "And if Pino decides he doesn't want to play along, it sounds like Aldo and his boss would make it dangerous for him. Anyway, I think it explains those cell phone numbers all over the world. I'll bet it's buyers or distributors."

"We'd better not stand around here whispering,"

said Rae. "We've got to get back to Manaus and get help."

"You're right. Let's get going."

They had all brought their flashlights, and Cody was sure that between the three of them, they could find their way back to camp. *If* they could get out of the compound, they had a chance—that is, *if* they could avoid any animals that didn't want to be friends on the way.

They had seen Aldo put the keys to the plane in a pouch. *If* Aldo had left the pouch at camp, maybe they could get back to Manaus. *If* he and Pino didn't get back to camp before they had a head start, that is. It was a lot of *ifs*.

The three made their way cautiously to the doorway. As they stood there looking for workers on patrol, several lights snapped off suddenly. Only one was left on, directly over the entrance gate. There was a worker stationed there. He was shouldering a rifle.

Cody could see Otis's face outlined in the darkness. He took Otis's hand and put it to his own throat. Did Otis understand what he meant?

Otis nodded. He knew that Cody had been practicing throwing his voice. He was pretty good at it. He waited for Cody's next move and prayed that it would work.

Cody took several deep breaths and tried to focus, the way the sensei had taught him in karate class. It wasn't easy to concentrate when you were so scared. He told himself that they were all depending on him. Then he took one more breath and . . .

Ow! Ow! Ow! The shrieks came from the corner of the building. The guard's head snapped in that direction. *Ow! Ow!* Two more shrieks sent him running that way.

Cody felt a wave of relief wash over him. It had worked. He had been practicing for months.

"Awesome, dude," Otis whispered. "Let's move."

In an instant, the three were through the gate and on their way into the jungle. They ran until the trees closed over them and their lungs were about to explode.

As they ran, Cody thought about the document he'd seen in the office and stuffed into his back pocket. It put Mr. Estevez in the middle of the whole business. It was hard for Cody to believe it. He hoped there was some explanation, but he could not imagine what it could be.

"Can you find the path, Cody?" asked Rae, panting.

"Right over here."

Otis and Rae followed Cody through the tangle of

trees. "Remember, don't step over any logs," said Rae. "That's where snakes often hide."

They followed the marked trees through the jungle. The chirping of the tree frogs grew louder. Suddenly a howl tore through the air. They all jumped. It was a howler monkey.

"Wait a minute," Otis said a moment later. He had heard something moving. "I think we're being followed. I don't think it's human, either. It's an animal."

"A jaguar? A panther?" Cody asked, snapping his words out.

"I'm not sure what it is."

Twigs snapped. There was a rustling sound and a kind of snuffling noise.

"It's never a good idea to run," whispered Otis. "Walk slowly."

They pressed on. But the rustling in the bushes got louder. *It* was getting closer. There was that snuffling noise again.

"Uh-oh," said Rae in a hushed voice. "Something is looking at us—and I don't like the glint in its eye."

"Its *eye*?" asked Otis.

"I can only see one. Oh—it's turning its head. There's another eye on the other side."

There was another loud rustling. Cody shined

his flashlight in the direction of the noise. They all watched in horror as a huge, dark animal burst through the trees. It had a thick body and short legs for its size—but it must have weighed nearly five hundred pounds. And it was thundering right toward them!

[Chapter Ten]

Cody, Otis, and Rae froze. The animal lurched toward them with a clumsy gait. But it was fast. As it sped closer, they could see it had a small head and a nose that looked like an anteater's.

It might have been the time to run, but none of them could move a muscle. Every knee felt like it was made of jelly.

"Do something, Otis. Do it *now*," Cody said through gritted teeth. If they ever needed Otis's "animal magic," it was now.

Otis could feel his heart pounding in his chest. He fought to calm down. He knew that animals could smell fear, and this creature was getting quite a whiff of it.

He exhaled slowly and kept his eyes focused on the animal. And then something happened that he didn't understand.

Suddenly, the animal stopped in its tracks. It turned

its head and gazed at them with one eye, turned the other way, and looked at them with the other eye. It took a step back, then another, and another. It shook its head. Then, it turned around and thundered off through the jungle.

"You did it, Otis," Cody said with relief.

"Oh, dudes, I am so glad that thing is gone," breathed Rae. "It was a tapir—kind of like a cross between a wild pig and an anteater."

Otis blinked. "Well, maybe I did it—and maybe we just got lucky. It's been known to happen. On the Lewis and Clark expedition a brown bear charged at Captain Lewis with its mouth wide open. But when it got near him it stopped and ran away. He never could figure out why."

"Well, tapirs *are* naturally shy," said Rae.

"You could have fooled me," said Cody.

"Native tribes hunt them and eat them sometimes," Rae said as she rubbed some dirt off her knees.

"Ew," said Cody. "Let's hope that's the fiercest animal we encounter tonight." He glanced at Otis and gave him a lopsided grin. "My brother the *tapir whisperer*." He chuckled.

"Cut it out," Otis said with a warning note in his voice. "Come on. Let's get a move on."

They walked on through the jungle, listening for

approaching animals. But the only noises they heard came from the chorus of tree frogs. Now and then a howler monkey let out an explosive yelp. It never failed to make them jump.

Finally they reached the clearing where they had made camp. A litter of young squirrel monkeys chattered happily as they climbed all over Otis's hammock. They chewed on the strings. In the tree above, the parents seemed to be screeching encouragement.

"Hey, get down from there, you guys!" Otis rocked the hammock, sending the monkeys flying into the air. They chattered louder as they landed on the ground and scampered up the tree trunks into the branches. The parents shrieked at Otis.

"Oh, hush up," he said as he began to untie the hammock. "Fun's over."

While Cody untied his hammock and Rae's, she looked for the pack where Aldo had put the keys. "Maybe he took it with him," she said after a moment.

"Keep looking," Cody said urgently. "If we can't find those keys, we're going to have a tough time getting back to Manaus."

"We could make a raft," Otis suggested.

"I found the keys!" Rae held them up. "I'll just put them back in the waist pack and strap it on."

"Good news," said Cody. "Come on, let's get our

stuff together. Make sure you don't forget anything we might need."

"We'd better hurry, too," said Otis. "It sounded like Pino was really concerned about us. But Aldo wasn't. We don't want to be anywhere near here when he shows up."

They packed up as quickly as they could. Backpacks shouldered, they set off trudging through the jungle. Otis checked his compass. "To get back to where the plane is, we should be heading southeast. I think we could make it by daylight."

"Let's just try to put as much distance between us and them as we can," said Rae. "I'll feel a lot better when we take off. Those flying lessons Uncle Vinnie gave you are going to pay off big time. By the way, which one of you is going to be the pilot?"

"I will," Cody and Otis both said at once. Then each one said, "No you won't. *I'm* going to fly the plane."

"Oh, come on, guys, don't start arguing," said Rae. "We've got to stick together. Let's flip a coin or something."

"Not now," Otis grumbled. "We'll figure it out later, when we get to the plane."

But as it turned out, things were decided long before they reached the plane. They had been walking for more than two hours when suddenly Otis let out the most bone-chilling scream that Cody and Rae had ever heard.

They both raced to his side. "What is it, Otis, what happened?"

Otis had fallen to the ground. He was clutching his leg and rolling from side to side. His face was contorted in agony. It was obvious that he was in too much pain to say a word.

Rae shined her flashlight all around him frantically. "Oh no!" she groaned. "I see a bullet ant. Look, Cody!"

In the beam of her flashlight, Cody saw a dark ant about an inch long crawling off toward a tree trunk. Without thinking he took a step backward.

"That's right," said Rae. "We should stay away from there. Bullet ants build nests at the base of trees. Let's pull Otis away. Maybe he brushed against one that was crawling up the trunk. I read that they don't sting unless they are threatened."

They both grabbed Otis by the shoulders and pulled him from the tree. He was moaning in pain.

"They call them *bullet* ants because their bite is supposed to be as painful as being hit by a bullet," said Rae. "It looks like that's true."

Cody looked at his brother and felt a wave of nausea. "I'm going to be sick," he said.

"Pull yourself together, Cody," Rae told him. "Otis is the one who's going to be sick—and feverish and in awful pain for the next three to five hours. Then he should keep getting better all through tomorrow but . . ."

"But what?"

"They call them *twenty-four-hour ants*, too, because it takes twenty-four hours for the pain to go away. Sometimes longer."

"He won't die, will he?" Cody's voice pleaded.

Rae put down her backpack and searched for a Benadryl. "Otis, swallow this," she said, pushing it between his lips. She handed him her bottle of water, and he took a sip.

"Oh, it hurts," he groaned. "I don't think I can walk."

"No, I don't think you can. I don't think you should try. We'd better camp here for awhile. Let's just try to get a little farther from that tree where the ant nest is."

Together Rae and Cody carried Otis a few yards away. Then they began stringing up the hammocks and mosquito netting.

Double Detectives

"It's a good thing we brought these with us," said Cody. "I was going to suggest we leave them because we were in such a hurry." He bit his lip. "I know Aldo will be looking for us, but Otis just can't go on right now."

Rae nodded.

By the time they were finished putting up the hammocks and nets, Cody and Rae were both feeling overcome with exhaustion. They lifted Otis into a hammock and then threw themselves into their own. They were both asleep in seconds.

Cody didn't know why, but several hours later he found himself wide awake. For a minute he didn't know where he was. Then the sounds of the chirping tree frogs sunk into his brain and he remembered where he was and what had happened. He glanced over at his brother. Otis was sleeping quietly. A look toward Rae told him that she, too, was sound asleep.

Then the skin on the back of his neck tightened. A chill gripped him in spite of the hot, humid blanket of the night. Two eyes were looking right at him. These eyes were human.

[Chapter Eleven]

The Chameleon had just received an e-mail from his contact in Brazil that made him furious. He flung his leopard-skin robe to the floor in a fit of rage. Those children should never have been allowed to get involved. If something happened to them, the police would start sniffing around.

On the other hand, if nothing happened to them, they would probably cause more trouble. He clenched his fists at his sides. Why was he surrounded by fools? If anything happened to his new business, they would all have to pay.

[Chapter Twelve]

Cody sat bolt upright and clutched his chest. His other hand gripped the side of his hammock. His heart was hammering with fear. When the man spoke to him he was nearly too astonished to breathe.

"Don't be afraid. I heard you moving in the forest. I want to help you."

The man was speaking to him in English. But his hair was worn in a bowl cut like many pictures of Amazon basin natives. He had the sharp, chiseled features of the people from the tribes, too. Around his neck was a necklace of feathers, but he was wearing a long-sleeved shirt and pants.

"Who are you?"

"I am Koobi."

Cody sat up and dangled his feet over the side of the hammock. "But who . . ."

"Don't be afraid. I am a member of the Pirahã tribe. Our village is not far away."

"So why do you speak English? And your clothes . . ."

"I'll explain later. The sun will be up soon. Your friend needs help. I can prepare some medicine that will help him walk. We can take him to my village and he can rest."

Cody thought it over. It didn't take him long. They needed help to stay away from Aldo, and maybe from Pino as well. What better place to hide than in the village of a native tribe?

"All right. Are you sure your medicine can help him?"

"I can prepare a poultice of plants that will help the swelling go down and make the fever go away. I know he was bitten by a bullet ant."

"But how did you know?"

"I saw the wound. I could feel his fever. My people have a lot of experience with insects of the forest. Trust me, I know what to do."

The man's voice was calm and sure. So after some more thought, Cody decided that the best thing to do was to trust him.

Koobi prepared his poultice of water and plants and placed it on Otis's wound. By the time the sun was on the horizon, Otis was able to stand and walk, leaning on Koobi.

Koobi led them to his village. It was a collection of huts made of poles with thatched roofs clustered at random. People were already up and about. They stared at the newcomers with wide, curious eyes.

It was easy to see that the Pirahã were not completely isolated from outside civilization. The women wore loose knee-length dresses. Some of the men wore loincloths, but many were wearing shorts. They had no shoes but their feet were hard and calloused. Many wore necklaces made of beads and feathers. No one was pierced or painted.

The children stared at Rae and the twins. But they weren't too shy to step right up and touch them. They put their little hands on the twins' faces and stroked Rae's hair.

"You must be hungry," said Koobi. "Have something to eat, and then nap a bit if you want. I know you didn't get much sleep."

"Thanks," said Cody, "but we really need to get home as soon as possible."

"That's right," Rae agreed. "The sooner we get going, the better."

"Why are you in such a hurry? Are your parents worried? And why are you traveling through the forest alone?"

"It's a long story." Cody felt his knees begin to

buckle. "Maybe we'd better eat something after all." His stomach growled loudly.

Koobi said something to the others. Soon Cody and Rae had plates of fish and manioc with bananas and a sweet fruit juice in front of them. A few feet away, someone was feeding Otis.

"Now," Koobi said, leaning forward with his elbows on his knees. "Why are you alone in the jungle, and why are you in a hurry?"

Cody and Rae both took an extra mouthful of food before answering. "It's because of endangered animals," Rae began. "We're staying with someone whose son is part of a smuggling operation."

"We left the son—his name is Pino—back there. They have a whole warehouse full of all kinds of animals," said Cody. "It's all high tech. Antibacterial washes and temperature controls. Pino seemed like he might be changing his mind about the whole thing, but that made this guy Aldo pretty mad. I think Pino might be in danger."

Koobi stroked his chin. "I know exactly what you are talking about. Some of these men have come to my people and asked them to catch animals for them. It is not something my people would do." He rubbed his forehead.

"They found others who would help them,

though," he went on. "They were tempted by the things the men showed them, the jewelry, the motion-picture cameras, and other things."

"I got a couple of pictures of the inside of the warehouse just before we left," Rae said.

"Smart girl." Koobi smiled. "If you have pictures, no one can say that the place isn't there."

Rae took a big gulp of juice. "Why were you in the jungle by yourself, anyway?"

"It's a lot safer for me than for you. I woke up and went walking to think. It's something I've done since I was a boy."

"You speak English, and the tribal language, too. How come?" asked Cody.

"Well, as you can see my tribe has had contact with the world outside the forest," he said. "Others speak English, but not as much as I do."

Koobi looked thoughtful. "When I was a little boy I walked off by myself into the rain forest. I must have been about four years old, and I was looking at animals. I saw a baby monkey who had wandered away from its mother."

He stopped talking for a moment to watch a little girl walking two baby armadillos as if they were puppies. For a moment she stared at Cody's freckled face and then kept walking.

"I lost sight of the monkey, and I got lost myself," Koobi went on. "I hadn't told my parents that I was leaving the village—so I don't know when they missed me. It was the next day when some people found me while they were rafting down the river. They tried for hours to find my village. They finally gave up. Not knowing what else to do, they took me into the boat and back to their home. They raised me until I grew up and went to college."

Cody and Rae both stopped eating. "What about your parents?" Cody asked.

"The people who cared for me wouldn't have known how to find them," said Koobi. "*They* became my parents, and they were very good to me. But after I finished college I felt that something was missing. I came back and found my Pirahã parents. Now I stay here sometimes and sometimes in Manaus."

"It must be so different. Like being in two worlds," said Cody.

"It is," Koobi agreed. "I've been working with the police to nail these animal smugglers. I never found the warehouse until tonight. But *you* were the ones who got inside."

Cody put down his plate. "I'm going to ask Otis if he's feeling well enough to travel. Then let's get going, okay?"

He walked over to where Otis lay in a hammock. "How you doin', dude?"

"A lot better." Otis grinned. "Still sore, but whatever Koobi put on that bite did the trick. I can't describe how it felt—like being bitten by a shark with hot knives for teeth."

Rae had crept up behind Cody and peered at Otis's leg. "Wow, you've got a big bruise."

"Compared to the way it felt before, the bruise feels great," Otis said. He smiled as he eased himself off the hammock. He took a couple of slow, careful steps, then a couple more that weren't so careful.

"How does it feel?" Koobi asked.

"Good enough," Otis said firmly. "Let's do this." He turned to his brother. "You get to fly the plane though, dude. I wouldn't trust this foot on the brake."

"Are you sure you can handle it?" Koobi asked Cody. "I can help you find the plane, but I can't fly it." He peered at Cody doubtfully. "Are you sure you can fly that plane? You seem awfully young to be a pilot."

Cody put his hands in his pockets. "Well, you probably know that I am too young to have a pilot's license. My brother and I are twelve years old. But I could get a license if I were a few years older. I have flown well over the forty hours required. I've passed the tests for student, sport, and recreational pilot. I am familiar with Cessnas—that's the plane they used to get us here."

"He's telling the truth," Otis said. "I studied piloting, too. One of our uncles has a school in Deerville, New York. That's where we live."

Koobi still looked doubtful. "You guys are twelve years old. How much experience flying solo do you have, Cody?"

Cody looked down at the ground. "Enough," he said. He looked up and glanced from Otis to Rae.

"Cody has had enough experience to fly us back to Manaus," said Rae. "He's not the type to play around."

"Watch me check out the plane," said Cody. "You'll see that I know what I'm doing."

Koobi shrugged. "Well, okay . . . I'll go get ready," he said, then walked away.

Cody exhaled a long breath. "Thanks for covering for me, guys. I think I can do this, but I wish I were a little more confident."

"Try to relax and concentrate," said Rae.

"You can do it," Otis said, punching him lightly on the arm. "Besides, you've got to. And I'll be right there with you."

Hours later, they were nearing their destination. As they approached the landing strip, Cody shielded his eyes from the sun.

"There is another plane beside ours," he said in a hushed voice. "I wonder who it belongs to. I wouldn't be surprised if it was more of Aldo's crew. We'd better be careful. They might be around."

"I don't think so," said eagle-eyed Otis. "The pilot is still in the cockpit. But he's tied up—and he's either sleeping or unconscious."

They hurried to the plane. The twins jumped inside.

The pilot's head lolled to the side and his hair fell over his eyes. His lips were cracked and bleeding and there were lots of bruises on his face. It looked as if he had been beaten.

After a moment, the man stirred and groaned. He shook the hair from his face and opened his eyes.

Cody and Otis gasped. It was Luis Estevez.

[Chapter Thirteen]

The twins gave Luis some water. He tried to speak, but he was in no shape to do much talking. They untied him and, with Koobi's help, got him into the waiting plane.

When Rae saw him, her eyes widened. "Someone gave him an awful beating," she said.

"I wonder what Luis was doing here," Otis said in a hushed voice. "We'll have to find out later. He's barely conscious."

"This whole situation is going from bad to worse." Cody ran a hand through his hair. He began moving around the plane, examining every part. He used the fuel cup to check for water in the tanks. Koobi never took his eyes off him.

"You've got me convinced that you know what you're doing," he murmured after a few moments. "Can you find the airport in Manaus?"

"I think so," Cody answered. "There should be a chart in the plane." He searched inside. "Got it."

"I remember that the airport for the private planes is called Amazonas," Koobi told him.

Cody unfurled the chart.

"It's here," Koobi said, pointing a finger.

Cody looked and nodded. He folded the chart and went to examine the wing flaps.

"Got much more to do before we leave?" Koobi asked.

"I'm done," Cody said, wiping his hands on his pants. "Let's go, everybody. Otis, sit in front with me and help out, okay?"

Cody climbed into the pilot's seat, adjusting it to move it closer to the steering column. He looked for the checklist in the door's side pocket where he had found the chart.

Every plane is supposed to carry a copy of a checklist. It shows all of the many items to be taken care of at all stages of the flight. The checklist wasn't in the side pocket.

He felt under the seat and came up empty-handed. He looked left and right. "Where is the checklist? Did Aldo take it with him?" he muttered. "That was dumb. What good would it do him outside the plane?" He'd have to remember the checks as best he could. There were a lot of them.

Cody checked to make sure all the doors were securely closed. "Are your seat belts on, everybody?"

"Seat belts on," they all answered.

"Right door closed and locked," said Otis.

Mentally, Cody went down the items to be checked before starting up. "Fuel valve *on*, brakes *on*, circuit breakers *check*, brakes *hold*, master switch *on* . . ."

"Well, here we go," he said finally. "I can't radio in to Control so I'm clearing myself for takeoff."

He started the engine and they all listened to the whir of the propeller. Cody pulled back on the throttle and the plane began to taxi down the runway.

Cody peered at the gauges and tried to remember more of the checklist. "Flight instruments *checked and set*, ammeter *check*, oil temperature *check* . . ." He moved the throttle forward for full power and applied some right rudder. Moments later, they watched as the nose went up and the plane lifted into the air.

The plane rose higher. The passengers listened as Cody muttered to himself. "Land light off . . . gauges checked . . . cruise set . . . 122 miles per hour . . ."

"You're *on top of things*," said Otis.

Cody groaned. "This is no time for puns, and that was really bad, by the way."

"How about a palindrome?"

"If this were a seaplane maybe I could land it in a *loopy pool*. There's one."

"Not one of your best."

"Well, *I* think it's still pretty good," Cody retorted.

Suddenly the plane began to bounce in the air. Koobi gripped the back of Cody's seat. "What's going on? Are you sure you know what you're doing?"

Cody didn't answer. He gripped the wheel tighter and adjusted a couple of gauges. The plane bounced harder. Cody made some more adjustments but the plane kept bouncing.

"Hey! What's going on?"

"Let him keep his mind on what he's doing," Otis said calmly. "We're being buffeted by updrafts. It's probably something to do with the moist, humid air. It's just a little turbulence, that's all."

"I can keep the plane steady," Cody told everyone firmly. "It will settle down once we get higher up."

"Speaking of landing, are you sure you know where you're going?" Koobi asked.

Cody looked at the gauges. "I sure do. I'm headed right for the Amazonas airport. Does everything look right to you, Otis?"

Otis checked the gauges himself. "It certainly does."

"Sorry, guys. The idea of being in a plane piloted by a twelve-year-old is just kind of unreal to me," Koobi mumbled.

"Well, Otis and I have had plenty of practice. We'll get there," Cody told him.

"I'm not worried about getting to the airport," said Rae after a moment. "I know Cody can get us there. It's what happens after that I'm worried about." She let out a sigh.

"You know something that really bothers me?" she went on. "It's how many of the Amazon rain-forest animals I've seen that weren't in the rain forest. They were in cages."

They were nearing the airport. Cody lowered the landing gear and made sure they were locked in place. Then he got on the radio.

"Control, this is Cessna two-three-one-niner-echo-tango approaching for landing."

The radio buzzed with static. Then they all heard the voice of an air traffic controller. "Cessna two-three-one-niner-echo-tango, you are clear for landing on runway one-four."

Cody banked the airplane and turned into the runway. He let the wing flaps down twenty degrees.

Then he lowered the speed to just under one hundred miles per hour and began the descent.

As Cody pointed the nose down and headed straight into the middle of the runway, the wheels touched down gently. He glided the plane to a stop.

Whew, he thought.

"You did a great job!" One of the air traffic controllers came to greet Cody. "I thought you sounded like a kid. How much flying have you done?"

"My brother and I have both had lots of lessons," Cody answered. "We need to speak with a customs agent."

When the traffic controller looked puzzled, Cody explained, "We have some evidence about illegally exporting animals."

"Look at this," Rae said. She held up her camera to show him the photos she had taken at the animal warehouse.

The traffic controller turned pale. "That animal looks sick."

"They have a pink dolphin, too," said Rae. "There are only about twelve hundred left in the wild. And some people kill them because they think their eyes and teeth have magical powers. It's terrible."

"It certainly is," said the traffic controller, whose name tag read J MARIO SOUZA. He looked at the other photos. "How could someone do this? So many animals—this is a big operation. I think we need the federal police. Come with me."

The traffic controller arranged for someone to drive the twins, Rae, and Luis to the office of the Polícia Federal in Manaus. Otis telephoned his dad and told him what had happened. By the time they got there, Mr. Carson and Maxim were waiting.

"Where is Mr. Estevez?" Cody asked his father. He was surprised that he hadn't come along.

Mr. Carson cleared his throat. "Mr. Estevez is at home recuperating from an accident," he said. "Shortly after you left, he went out to run an errand and was struck by a speeding car. It was a hit and run."

Rae and the twins gasped. "Is he all right?" Cody asked.

Mr. Carson nodded. "He suffered a slight concussion, but the doctors say he's going to be fine."

"Have they caught the person who hit him?" Rae asked.

"No," said Maxim. "Mr. Estevez doesn't even remember being hit, and the police don't have any leads. Apparently the street was practically deserted. One person said the car was brown, another said it was black, and that's it. Anyway, we'd better get Luis to a hospital."

They arrived at the mansion later to find Mr. Estevez in the study, attended by Carlos Santos. He had a bruise on his left temple but otherwise looked all right.

Mr. Estevez was lying on a sofa, his head propped up with pillows. When they entered the room, he sat up. "Now, tell me what this is all about," he said. "Why would anyone beat up Luis?"

The twins launched into the story. "Luis whispered *blackmail*," Otis told him. "He didn't say anything else, except his name."

Mr. Estevez listened as Otis and Cody told him the rest of the story. He looked more and more haggard and disappointed. "How could Pino get involved in such a business?" he asked incredulously, his mouth puckered in disgust.

"Well—maybe Pino didn't realize what he was getting into," said Cody. He told Mr. Estevez about the argument they had overheard in the warehouse.

"We're afraid that if Pino tries to back out of this business he could be in danger," said Otis.

Carlos was a grayish shade of pale. "This is a horror," he said. "Luis went to find Pino to tell him about their father's accident. I tried to stop him, but he wouldn't listen. I wish . . ."

Before he could say another word, the shrill sound of the doorbell shattered the air. Moments later, the maid appeared. A uniformed man was with her. She introduced him as Captain Ricardo Montez of the police department.

"May I speak to you, Mr. Carson?" he asked.

"Of course."

"I hate to ask you this question," he said, "but I've talked it over with my supervisor and we agree that it's the only way. May we take Cody with us to show us the way to the warehouse? I really don't like the idea of taking a kid on a dangerous mission. But I don't see how we can find that warehouse without him. You're his father, though, and the decision is up to you."

"*If* Cody goes, I'm going along with him," said Mr. Carson.

"But . . ." Captain Montez began.

"The only way he is going is if I go along as well," Mr. Carson said firmly.

"Why can't I go, too?" Otis blurted out. Then he winced. That bite still hurt.

"I should also come along," announced Maxim. "I have acquired a great variety of knowledge that you'd undoubtedly find useful."

Mr. Estevez spoke up from the sofa. "My son is involved—perhaps I should go, too."

Captain Montez had been narrowing his eyes more and more. Now he let out an explosive burst of air. "Well, why don't we *all* go?" he said, and snorted. "Why don't we invite the maid along, and everyone else you know. Let's make it a party."

Captain Montez regained his usual dignified manner. "It was Cody who flew the plane, so it's logical for him to come with us," said Captain Montez. "But it would be irresponsible to take more civilians than we absolutely have to. We can't keep track of them, or protect them. We'll have Cody guide one of our pilots."

"I can fly the plane," Cody protested. "I did it before."

Captain Montez shook his head. "You did well in an emergency, son. But remember, you don't have a pilot's license. We'll have an officer fly the plane." He turned to Mr. Carson. "Well, what do you say, sir? We'll be careful with him."

"As I said before, Captain Montez, if Cody goes, I

go," said Mr. Carson. He turned to Koobi. "Can you remember the way?"

Koobi shook his head. "If we were walking through the rain forest, I could. But not by air. Cody knows the way to fly."

"I know the way through the forest, too," said Cody. "I paid attention when Koobi led us to the airstrip. I can find our camp. I marked the trees along the trail to the warehouse."

Mr. Carson looked at his son. "Do you want to do this, Cody?"

"Absolutely."

Mr. Carson hesitated. "Then let's go." He looked Captain Montez in the eye. "I want Cody kept safe."

"You have my word," Captain Montez told him.

✳

Cody waited while the captain made some phone calls. Captain Montez quickly put together a posse. Then they headed for the airport.

Cody prayed that he could lead the police back to the warehouse.

[Chapter Fourteen]

The Chameleon's eyes were as small and flat as dimes on the surface of his face. Now they were squeezed shut tightly. He pounded on his computer keyboard with his fist. The e-mail he had just received sent a white-hot flash of anger through his veins.

Blackmail wasn't part of his plan. At least, not yet. Someone had tried to do some business on his own. Obviously one of those sneaky, snivelling airstrip guards. The goon had mistaken Luis Estevez for his brother, Pino. Now there was another reason for the police to come nosing around.

When he found out which guard had roughed up Luis, he was going to punish him. The Chameleon picked up a corner of his leopard-skin robe and twisted it viciously.

[Chapter Fifteen]

"The trail looks different in the daylight," Cody said. He had managed to lead the police to the landing strip.

"I told you that we shouldn't have sent a kid," said one of the officers, whose name was Fernando Bezerra. He had been making remarks from the beginning of the flight.

Cody was glad that his dad was at the end of the line of officers. Bezerra had been calling Cody "kid" or "kiddo," and he didn't want his dad to hear it. From the tone of his voice, Bezerra might as well have called Cody a toddler. Cody didn't like it, and he knew his father wouldn't either.

Bezerra had been quiet for a little while, but soon he spoke up again. "The police department is no place for children. We aren't here to play. We're here to do a job. That's right, isn't it?"

If he was waiting for one of the other officers to

go along with him, he was wasting his time. They all were silent.

Cody had been holding his tongue. But he had had enough. He whirled and faced the officer. Although he was angry, he made sure to speak calmly and politely.

"Excuse me, sir. I'm aware that we aren't playing childish games. I'm the one leading the police to the warehouse and I'd appreciate some respect," he said evenly.

"*Woooo!*" The other officers sounded approval. Bezerra glared at Cody. "Are you going to let him speak to me like that, Captain Montez?" he asked. Captain Montez stroked his chin. "It seems to me that this boy managed to find the warehouse, get away, fly a plane, and lead us back here. Cody, can you take us to the warehouse?"

"He'll get us lost," Bezerra protested. "He just said everything looks different in the daylight."

"Officer Bezerra, I was speaking to Cody. Once again, can you take us to the warehouse, Cody?"

Cody glanced at Bezerra. Then he said, "Yes, sir, I can do it. I marked the trees on the trail with my Swiss Army knife. All I have to do is follow the marks."

He gave Officer Bezerra a hard look. "Things look different in the daylight, but it doesn't matter."

"Okay, then," said Captain Montez. "Listen to me, everyone. Right now the only chance we have of finding the animal warehouse is this young man. What's most important about that is we may need his help to rescue Pino Estevez. So for now, any *childish* remarks about his age will stop. Understood?"

Most of the officers said *yes* and a few added an enthusiastic *all right*, but Officer Bezerra pressed his lips into a thin line. When Captain Montez kept looking at him, he turned his head and stared off into the distance.

"Is it understood, Officer Bezerra?" Captain Montez prompted finally.

Officer Bezerra puffed out his cheeks and blew out the air. "Yes, sir," he said. It was obvious that he didn't like saying it.

At the end of the line, Mr. Carson had caught wind of a ruckus. "What's going on there, Cody?" he called.

"Nothing, Dad, it's all taken care of," Cody called back.

As he kept on walking, Cody thought about Officer Bezerra. The man's attitude just didn't make any sense at all. No matter how he felt about young people, he had to understand that Cody was the only one who could lead Captain Montez to the warehouse. The only other way to locate it would be to spot it from the air, and the trees made that impossible.

Why did Officer Bezerra hate having him along so much? Then a thought occurred to Cody. Maybe Bezerra didn't want him along because he didn't want anyone to find the warehouse. Maybe he was on the wrong side of the law.

It certainly was possible. Having a police officer working with you when you were trafficking animals couldn't hurt. And there was a lot of money in the illegal business. Plenty to give some to an officer who was willing to take a bribe.

Then he wondered . . . if Bezerra was involved, just how far would he go to stop the men from finding the warehouse?

They walked on. Cody found the camp. "Now I'll start looking for the trail marks," he announced. "We'll find that warehouse for sure."

They all kept walking. Cody found one of his trail marks on a tree. Then he found another and another and another.

"I know we're on the right track," he told the officers. "It shouldn't be much farther now. Keep walking on this path. I've got to go for a minute . . . y'know . . . nature calls . . ."

"Go ahead, you don't have to explain, Cody," said Captain Montez. "We'll all slow down."

Cody left the path and walked a few yards into the dense woods. The moment he stopped, someone grabbed him from behind and clamped a hand over his mouth.

"Keep quiet," the man's voice said harshly.

Cody recognized Officer Bezerra's voice. His mind started racing. *Why didn't I hear him?* he wondered.

The officer had crept up behind him without making a sound. Now Cody nodded to let him know that he wouldn't scream. He could probably have used karate to get free and then run back to the group, but he wanted to hear what Bezerra had to say.

Slowly, Officer Bezerra took his hand off Cody's mouth. "Listen to me, kid," he said. "You don't want the police to find that warehouse."

"I think I do," said Cody. "I think the police want to find it, too. It seems like *you're* the one who doesn't want it to be found. Why don't you want to save a lot of animals from being mistreated?"

"Oh, you're worried about animals being mistreated, are you?" Bezerra said with a sneer in his voice. "What's wrong with living in a zoo—or being a pet?"

"They aren't free. They're wild animals. They're supposed to be free."

Officer Bezerra snorted. "Free to be eaten by another animal? The animals are kept in clean cages. They're fed well and given water. What's wrong with that?"

"What happens to them after they leave the place? Why don't you want them to be freed?"

"You're all mixed up, kid. This is a breeding farm. The only animals for sale are animals bred in captivity. They only sell the offspring."

"That's a lie," said Cody. "Even if it were true, it would still mean that wild animals are caged up. It's a lot easier to just poach wild animals than breed them. *That's* what's going on."

Officer Bezerra stamped his foot. "Why can't you understand, kid? This thing makes a lot of money. These animals are worth big bucks."

"So what?"

"Um—I'll tell you so what," he said. "Do you want to make a lot of money? Want to buy you and your brother a couple of ponies? Want to take some trips to Disney World? How about if you could take your dad on a trip to Europe? Wouldn't you like to buy all the games you want?"

Cody was getting angrier and angrier. Who did this guy think he was? He was acting like he was talking to a toddler. What kind of a police officer was he to offer someone a bribe?

He gritted his teeth and forced himself to calm down. He was going to let Captain Montez take care of this. He played along.

"Okay. How much money are we talking about? Enough for lots of vacations and a racecar?"

"Ha! Yeah, kid. Enough for lots of vacations. Enough for a racecar. Now you're getting smart. I'll tell you what. I'm going to talk to the guy I work for and explain what you've done for us. I know he'll give you lots of money. All you have to do is get lost. All of a sudden you can't remember where you're going any-more, okay? Nobody will blame you. After all, you're just a kid."

There was that word again—and that annoying tone. Cody gritted his teeth. "Great. Can I be alone for a minute now?" he said.

"Oh—sure, kid. I'll go on ahead. Just hurry up." Then Officer Bezerra was gone.

Moments later, Cody caught up with the officers. He saw Bezerra turn green as he marched right up to Captain Montez.

"Officer Bezerra just tried to bribe me," he whispered. "He promised me a lot of money if I'd lose the way to the animal warehouse."

Captain Montez clenched his jaw. "I've been afraid of something like this. We've been watching Officer Bezerra for months now. We've followed him and seen him meeting people suspected of being involved in animal trafficking. We've seen him taking money from them. We just needed one more piece of evidence."

"Are you going to arrest him?"

"Yes."

"What if he isn't the only one?" Cody asked.

"You're using your head, young man. However, I'm glad to say that I trust my men. There are more good officers than bad apples."

Captain Montez stopped walking. "Halt!" he ordered the men. "I'm sorry to say that one of the officers in this group is not on our side. Officer Bezerra, you are under arrest."

"On what charge?" Bezerra protested.

"This boy says you tried to bribe him," replied Captain Montez.

"Then it's his word against mine," Bezerra protested. "You can't arrest me based on what that boy says."

"I'm sorry, Bezerra," said Captain Montez. "I already have surveillance photos of you taking money from people suspected of animal trafficking. I'm arresting you on suspicion of transporting endangered animals. I should have arrested you before. . . . I just wanted to give you the benefit of the doubt. I've always trusted my men—but this time I was wrong."

Captain Montez walked toward Officer Bezerra. He snapped handcuffs on his wrists.

By then Mr. Carson and the other officers had caught up with the group. Mr. Carson caught Cody's eye and gave him a thumbs up.

[Chapter Sixteen]

Cody stayed away from Officer Bezerra for the rest of the way. Bezerra was taken to the back of the line, where Mr. Carson had returned. Cody's father kept glaring at him.

Cody walked up front with Captain Montez. But he could almost *feel* the heat of Bezerra's anger at his back.

He followed the trail markings that he had made with his Swiss Army knife. The trail began to look more and more familiar. Soon they were looking at the yard of the warehouse surrounded by the chain-link fence.

Neither one of the guards wanted any trouble. As soon as they saw the uniforms of the police officers, they threw down their guns and put up their hands.

"Thank you, Cody," said Captain Montez. "We'd never have found this place without you. It's completely covered with trees. It's amazing how huge it is."

"Wait until you see what's inside," said Cody. "You'll be knocked out."

The captain was knocked out all right. So were the other officers.

"I've seen enough," said the captain after he inspected the room with the animal stalls and the temperature-controlled rooms. He told the officers to watch the outside entrances. Then he marched into the office. There he found a public address system and flicked the switch.

"Attention, all personnel," he said. "This is Captain Montez of the federal police. Everyone here must walk into the yard and surrender to one of the officers. You will all be placed under arrest. Do not resist or try to run. My officers are guarding the entrances."

Soon they heard feet shuffling in the corridor. Moments later, ten men were standing in different parts of the yard. An inspection by the captain revealed that Aldo and Pino were missing.

Captain Montez soon discovered that no amount of questioning would get the men to reveal their whereabouts. He suspected it was because of Aldo.

"I suppose we're going to have to search the building," Captain Montez said wearily. He motioned to two officers and asked them to follow him back inside.

Then Cody spotted Aldo sneaking toward the gate. "There he is!" he cried.

While police officers set off in pursuit, Cody went back into the warehouse. He knew that his father would wonder where he was, and that he'd be worried. But he had to find Pino. He crept through the long hallway with rooms on either side. When he passed the office, he noticed that the computer inside had been shattered. There would be nothing to find inside it now.

Cody kept on walking, checking each room for Pino. It didn't take long to find him. Pino was in a room with long metal tables that looked like some sort of laboratory. He was gagged and tied to a chair.

Cody removed his gag and undid the knots on the ropes. Pino stood up slowly and rubbed his wrist. "Thanks." He made a sweeping gesture. "Look at this place," he said. "It's for making new designer species. They are planning to genetically engineer snakes with unusual markings, glow-in-the-dark mice, stuff like that. It's real science fiction. These people are nuts."

Cody gulped. "Yeah."

"It's a good thing you arrived when you did," Pino said. "Aldo was about to take some animals on a trip. Come with me."

Cody followed Pino to the shipping area. On a long table, a suitcase was open. Rows of iguanas were crammed inside like sardines.

"Let's put these babies back in one of the cages," he said. "They need food and water. They can be released later."

"I guess you and Aldo had a disagreement," Cody observed.

"Yeah, you could say that," Pino said gruffly. "I finally came to my senses and told him I couldn't be a part of this anymore. That really ticked him off. But when I told him he couldn't take those animals in the suitcase, he really went berserk."

"My brother and I just got our black belts in karate, but I wouldn't have wanted to tangle with Aldo."

"That's smart of you, Cody. Aldo is a black belt, too. He's also *really* strong. I've seen him fight. It's like the guy doesn't even feel pain. We've put you in enough danger already." Pino ran a hand through his hair and exhaled a burst of air.

"I owe you an apology," said Pino. "We should

never have left you all out there in the rain forest alone. It was irresponsible and stupid. One of many irresponsible and stupid things I've done in the past couple of years. But that's all over now."

Together they walked out into the yard. When Mr. Carson spotted Cody, he hurried over and put a hand on his shoulder. "Well done, son," he said.

Aldo was in handcuffs, standing beside Captain Montez. He gave Pino and Cody an evil look. Then he spat on the ground.

[Chapter Seventeen]

The police questioned Aldo for hours. He admitted nothing. He kept insisting that he operated a breeding farm that supplied pet stores and zoos, and that he had done nothing illegal. None of the others who had been arrested were talking either. They had all clammed up tight.

Captain Montez became frustrated and then exhausted. He didn't believe Aldo for an instant. And he didn't believe Aldo was the mastermind of the organization, as he kept saying he was. To pull off an operation the size of the one in the warehouse, someone would have to be a heavy hitter in the crime world. It had to be someone with plenty of money and plenty of connections. For whatever reason, Aldo was protecting somebody.

Captain Montez loved animals and hated seeing them mistreated in any way. He was horrified by what he had seen at the warehouse, even though the animals there were kept in clean, comfortable conditions. He knew enough about animal smuggling to know that such good environments were the exception. Most of the time, the animals were kept in small, filthy cages. Often they were poorly fed and sometimes abused.

Who knows what happened to them when they left the warehouse? Some were stuffed into suitcases to be smuggled into airports. Others were hidden in clothing or in crates under merchandise or animals legal to export.

And what happened when they reached their destinations? Were they sold to people who would care for them well? Maybe not. Maybe they would even be killed.

And sending these animals into other countries could endanger thousands of other creatures. If one carried a disease, it could spread and become an epidemic. If people ate infected animals, such as chickens, they could die.

Captain Montez also realized that the animal smugglers preyed on people, too. Some of the poor people who helped capture the animals were struggling to get by. While others were just greedy and cruel, some only wanted to feed their families.

Montez sank into a chair behind his desk and put his head in his hands. If only that computer hadn't been smashed. Maybe they could have found some information leading to who was running this illegal organization, and how to find him. Now, with no one talking, he and his officers had reached a dead end.

[Chapter Eighteen]

Cody awoke the next morning feeling better than he had in days. He had never in his life been as exhausted as when he got back to the mansion the night before. He yawned and stretched. The animal-trafficking operation had been exposed. Pino was out on bail. But the mystery was far from solved.

He still had to decide what to do about Mr. Estevez and the document he had found in the warehouse office. He had forgotten all about it until he felt it crinkle when he took off his pants to get into bed last night. When he read it more carefully, he realized that it put Mr. Estevez in the middle of the whole nasty animal smuggling business.

He wanted to find out who was behind the attempts on Mr. Estevez's life. And he really needed to find out who was the mastermind of the organization. Captain Montez had phoned last night and told

Mr. Estevez that he was sure that Aldo was protecting someone. Cody didn't believe that Aldo was in charge any more than Captain Montez did.

He threw back the covers and put his feet on the floor. "We've got our work cut out for us," he muttered as he threw on some clothes. He chewed his lip. He knew his father and Maxim would tell them to leave matters to the police. But once he, Otis, and Rae discovered a mystery, they couldn't leave it alone.

Cody headed downstairs and found everyone gathered around the table in the garden. Luis had joined them, badly bruised but sitting straight and tall.

"Where are Koobi and Pino?" he asked.

"Koobi left last night while you were asleep," said Carlos, pouring Cody a glass of iced tea. "He said he had to get back to his tribe. Pino won't come out of his room."

"I guess Koobi has decided the life he wants," Luis said, twirling his glass between his hands. He looked at his father. "Maybe you should let Pino do that, sir," he said.

"Yes, yes, yes," Mr. Estevez said wearily. "I had a long talk with Pino last night. What he had to say was very interesting."

"He told you that he got involved in this animal-trafficking business to make money to go to art school," said Luis. "Isn't that right?"

Mr. Estevez threw down his napkin. "You knew about this?" he said, spitting out the words.

Luis sighed. "Not at first. Later on, I could tell that something was the matter with him. He didn't know what he was getting into, Father. But he didn't think he could talk to you. He wants so much for painting to be his life."

A hummingbird flew over the table, its wings beating so fast that they were a blur of motion. It hovered over a flower.

"Silly boy," said Mr. Estevez. "I'm offering him a great future in the coffee business. Why can't he see that, the way you do, Luis?"

"Because *he* doesn't want to be in the coffee business, Dad," said Luis. "He wants to be a painter."

Mr. Estevez waved his hand dismissively. "Look, son, painting pictures is fine for a hobby, but it's not a way to make a living," Mr. Estevez said.

"Mr. Carson makes a living from his art," Luis protested. "Why can't Pino try to do the same?"

Mr. Estevez sighed. "Mr. Carson has a great talent," he began. "Just look at my portrait. He's captured the real me."

They all turned to look at the finished portrait, which rested on an easel near the table. Mr. Estevez was wearing a suit and tie, seated in a chair in his study. He looked the part of a powerful executive, confident and in control.

"How do you know that Pino doesn't have great talent?" Luis snapped.

Mr. Estevez stamped his foot. "A great talent isn't always enough. Some people have great talent and are never recognized. They struggle all their lives. They are always poor. That isn't what I want for either of you."

"Take a look at Pino's paintings, Dad," Luis pleaded. "You haven't seen them in years. Every time he asks you to look at them, you refuse. Please, Father." He got up from the table. "Let's go to his studio."

"I'd like to see them," Mr. Carson said eagerly.

Mr. Estevez got to his feet. "Okay, if that's what you say, my friend. Let's go."

Luis led the way to Pino's studio, which stood behind the house. He unlocked the door and they all stepped inside. When they saw the paintings on the walls they were speechless.

Directly across from the door was a painting at least six feet by six feet of a tiger that looked out at them. The animal was so realistic, they could almost see him leaping off the canvas.

111

Most of the other paintings were scenes of monkeys, apes, and baboons. They scampered through the jungle, played together, cared for their babies.

"These are awfully good," said Mr. Carson.

"Yes, yes," Maxim agreed, eyeing them critically. "Quite extraordinary, really."

"This is what Pino wants, Dad," said Luis. "To paint pictures. Try to understand."

"You think I don't understand? I'm going to show you something. Come back to the house with me," said Mr. Estevez.

When they were all seated in the garden again, Mr. Estevez left and came back with two huge manila envelopes. They were stained and torn and faded with age. He opened them and began taking out black-and-white photographs. "These are some pictures I took a long time ago. I liked to photograph people. There are several pictures of your mother here."

Mr. Estevez showed them photos of a beautiful young woman with dark, sparkling eyes. "That is just how I remember her," said Luis. "She was always so happy."

"That is how I remember her, too," said Mr. Estevez.

"You never said anything about taking photographs, Dad. Why not?"

Mr. Estevez looked thoughtful. "I just put the idea away," he said. "I thought of being a photographer myself. It was when I started dating your mother. She thought I was very talented. But then . . ."

"But what, Dad?" asked Luis.

"But then your mother and I got married, and soon I found that we were going to have two sons. I couldn't pay the bills taking pictures. So I got a job as a salesman for a coffee company."

"And you threw away your dreams," said Luis.

"No, no, I didn't, son. At first that is what your mother said, too. But I found out that I liked the coffee business. Soon I opened my own store, and after a while I had my own fields and my own business. I found that I really enjoyed it. And it's a lot easier than being a poor photographer. Look around you. The coffee business built all this."

"I wish that I had seen these pictures before, Dad," said Luis.

Cody looked over the photos again. Mr. Estevez had signed every one in the right-hand corner. An idea was beginning in his head with a whisper that got louder and louder. Then it finally dawned on him.

That's it. The signature. The signature is the key.

Without a word he left the table and hurried to his room. The filthy pants he had worn in the rain forest were flung on a chair. He reached into the back pocket and pulled out the piece of paper he had taken from the office. Then he raced back to the dining room.

The others were still gathered around the table. When they saw him come running up, they stared in surprise.

Cody waved the piece of paper. "Mr. Estevez, I have a bill of sale deeding a parcel of your rain-forest land to Mr. Aldo Aldorado. And it has your signature on it."

Cody put down the bill of sale in front of Mr. Estevez. The man examined it and turned pale. He shook his head.

"I found the bill of sale in Aldo's warehouse. The signature puts you in the middle of Aldo's trafficking business. It looks like you hid the fact that you sold Aldo the land because you knew that he was going to use it for something illegal."

"That's not my signature," Mr. Estevez said, his voice barely above a whisper. "I would never sell that land. How can you think that I would be involved in Aldo's trafficking business? This is a forgery."

"I believe you," said Cody.

[Chapter Nineteen]

A heavy silence hung over the group. Cody looked thoughtful.

"Mr. Estevez, did you get your latest bank statement yet with the recent checks that have been cashed?"

"Why yes, it's in my desk," he said, looking surprised.

"Could I see one of those canceled checks, please? The one made out to Aldo for his work in the garden?"

Mr. Estevez hesitated. "You want to see my bank statement? *And* a canceled check to Aldo?"

"Cody, that is personal business," Mr. Carson said in a reproving tone.

"I have a good reason, Dad," said Cody. "Believe me, I'm not nosing into Mr. Estevez's finances."

"Oh, I suppose it's all right," Mr. Estevez said.

"I'll get it," Carlos volunteered.

"No, no, that's all right, Carlos. Please bring us

some pastry. I'll get the statement." Mr. Estevez went to his study and returned with an envelope.

Cody fumbled through it and pulled out a check. He laid it flat on the table. Then he placed the bill of sale on top. Everyone gathered around to watch what he was doing. The signatures matched up perfectly.

Otis understood right away. He slapped his brother on the back. "Way to go, Cody! You figured it out!"

"*I did, did I?*" Cody grinned at Otis, knowing his brother would catch the palindrome.

The others waited for Cody's explanation.

"A signature is never exactly the same from one time to the next. Mr. Estevez didn't sign this bill of sale because Aldo forged it, using the check from Mr. Estevez."

Carlos brought in a tray of pastries and set them on the table. He looked at Mr. Estevez's face and his eyes clouded with concern.

Mr. Estevez looked pinched and worn. "How is this possible? I am surrounded by crooks." He put a hand to the side of his face and looked at Cody.

"Forging my signature—I could have been in terrible trouble. What if no one had thought about the check given to Aldo? Unless he confessed, the authorities might not have discovered the forgery. I could have been proved an accomplice and sent to jail.

Not to mention the loss of my land. Thank you, Cody, very much."

"I couldn't have done it without Otis and Rae. We all suspected there was something going on almost from the moment we got here. The three of us have been piecing clues together all along the way."

Mr. Carson stroked his chin as he looked at Mr. Estevez. "I think we'd better take these items to the police," he said, picking up the check and the bill of sale. "After that, maybe you and I should have a talk about Pino's future."

"Oh, I think he's right," said Maxim, following them through the doors to the dining room. "Pino is very talented."

"At last, some good news," murmured Luis, heading out after them.

When the others had gone, Cody, Otis, and Rae helped themselves to pastries. "The portrait is finished, and our holiday is almost over," said Rae, biting into a fruit tart.

"It wasn't exactly a holiday, if you ask me," said Cody.

"Not entirely."

Carlos puttered around, gathering up plates and cups and glasses. "Poor Mr. Estevez," he said. "Having a son mixed up in animal trafficking. Imagine, they're even engineering new species out in that warehouse. Designer snakes, indeed. Whoever buys these animals is sick, that's all I have to say."

Carlos's little marmoset ran along the garden wall and jumped onto his shoulder. "Hello, *bebezinha*," the butler cooed. "That means *little baby*," he said. Then he fed the monkey a piece of pastry.

Cody stared at the butler and his pet. Something was definitely bothering him, but he couldn't figure out what it was.

[Chapter Twenty]

After breakfast, Cody and the others went upstairs to their rooms. Even though they were visiting and there were plenty of servants, Mr. Carson and Maxim insisted that they should neaten their rooms and make their own beds.

Cody picked up the pair of dirty pants that had held the bill of sale and started to throw them in the laundry hamper. A yellow scrap of paper fell out. He picked it up and examined it.

There was a word scribbled on it—*macquinho.* It reminded him of something. He figured that the yellow note must have been stuck to the bill of sale.

His brain began to hum. What did it want him to know?

Cody glanced outside and saw Carlos riding his bike up the walkway toward the street. The little monkey clung to his back.

Cody turned away from the window. "*Was it a rat I saw?*" he muttered, using a classic palindrome.

"Huh?" asked Otis.

The humming in Cody's brain grew louder. He turned to Otis and held out the yellow note. "I found this in the office at the warehouse," he said. "It was in the drawer under the computer, along with the forged bill of sale. What do you make of it?"

Otis took the yellow note and stared at the word. "Sometimes people keep passwords on scraps of paper under desk blotters—or in desk drawers," he said. "*Macquinho* means *little monkey* in Portuguese. Pino told me one day when Carlos was talking baby-talk to his little marmoset."

Cody and Otis exchanged knowing glances.

"Where is Carlos's room?" Otis whispered.

"It must be upstairs with the other servants' rooms," Cody replied. "Let's go."

They hurried upstairs and located Carlos's room. They found a bill addressed to him on his desk alongside his computer. Cody sat down and booted up.

The user name C. Santos appeared on the screen. Underneath was a prompt asking for the password. Cody's fingers shook as he typed in *macquinho*. He held his breath.

A magenta home page with a diamond-patterned

background appeared. Rows of icons filled the right side of the screen. "This looks just like the home page I saw on the computer screen in the office at the warehouse," Cody said with excitement.

"I'll bet this is a virtual private network and Carlos is a registered user. The computer at the warehouse was smashed, but we can access the records on the network from this one." He clicked on documents and began perusing folders.

"Look at this, Otis! There are lists of customers, distribution locations, personnel. This is a gold mine."

"I'll say," Otis agreed. "Take a look at his e-mail."

Cody accessed Carlos's e-mail program and found loads of incriminating correspondence. There were e-mails between him and Aldo about animal smuggling, and other e-mails to various parts of the world. Many of them were sent to someone in Indonesia—someone Carlos referred to as "The Chameleon."

On Carlos's hard drive, Cody found photos of Pino at the warehouse. It seemed that Aldo and the airstrip guard were not the only ones with blackmail on their minds.

"We've got to call Captain Montez right away," said Otis. "Grab that laptop."

Carlos walked into the great entrance hall and closed the door quietly. "I've enjoyed living in this house," he murmured under his breath.

Cody stepped out from the study doorway. "Why would you leave, then? Is it something to do with someone called The Chameleon?"

Carlos's mouth fell open. "What are you talking about?" he snapped.

"Just something we found on your computer." Otis appeared behind Cody. "Or rather, a lot of things we found on your computer. You're really involved in this Chameleon guy's business. Why don't you tell us about it?"

Carlos glanced over his shoulder. The little monkey leaped onto the dining room table, grabbed a piece of fruit, and began eating it as she stared at them all.

A sneer formed on Carlos's face. "Nosy boys playing detective. You have no idea what you've gotten tangled up in. I scouted out Mr. Estevez's land in the rain forest as the perfect place for The Chameleon to build his animal warehouse. Now I only had to find a way to make him sell the land." His smile was anything but friendly.

"When I found out that his son wanted to go to art school and that his father had a problem with it,

I began to form a plan. It should have been perfect." He scowled.

"First, I made sure that Aldo and Pino met and became friends. Aldo suggested that Pino help with transporting some animals for money. He told Pino he could save enough to go to school and he wouldn't have to depend on his father."

"Go on, there's more," said Otis.

"You're right, my young sleuth." Carlos nodded. "We offered Pino more money if he could convince his dad to sell to our cattle farmer. Of course, there was no farmer. It was Aldo who called Mr. Estevez and tried to pressure him into making a sale."

"Mr. Estevez was more stubborn than you thought he would be, wasn't he?" Cody said. "That's when he began having trouble with speeding cars."

"You boys are smarter than I gave you credit for," Carlos remarked. "Yes, with Mr. Estevez's signature on the bill of sale, we didn't need to negotiate anymore. We just needed him out of the way."

Carlos brushed a piece of lint off his shirt. "Pino never knew what he was getting into. We even planned to get a little more money by forcing him to buy our silence. It was Aldo's idea to threaten to tell his father about his involvement in animal trafficking. Pino never would have wanted him to know."

"But an airstrip patrol came up with the same idea," Otis said. "Only he thought Luis was Pino."

"Yes, he made a big mistake." Carlos crossed his arms. "He's very sorry now, I can assure you. And now, my young detectives, we have talked enough. Before you have a chance to tell anyone about this, I'll be halfway around the world with a brand-new identity."

Carlos swept past Cody and Otis and entered the study. He walked toward the desk where his computer lay but stopped short. He found himself surrounded by Captain Montez and several of his officers, along with Mr. Estevez.

"Sorry, Carlos," said Captain Montez. "What I've heard is very interesting. Besides, after Cody called, I had you followed. It seems that you went to the bank and withdrew a great deal of money from Mr. Estevez's account . . . by forging his signature on a check."

"Why did you do this?" asked Mr. Estevez.

"Money," Carlos said, his voice full of contempt. "But that isn't all. I hated your arrogance. I've seen people like you all my life. You push other people around. Look at all of the work I did for you—and yet you never wanted to give me a raise. Then the man known as The Chameleon approached me. He was interested in your land. I could get money and get back at you at the same time."

"Your reasoning is twisted, Carlos," said Captain Montez. "You're under arrest," he pronounced, as he snapped handcuffs on Carlos. As the police led Carlos out of the house, he glanced at the monkey that was still munching on fruit. "Good-bye, *macquinho*," he whispered.

When he reached the door, Carlos jerked to a halt. "How did you figure it all out, Cody?" Carlos asked, without turning around.

"Oh . . . I didn't right away. But you mentioned engineering new species at the warehouse. I never said anything about that. The only way you could have known is if you were involved in the business. Then there was the word *macquinho*. You were always calling your monkey little pet names, including the one that Aldo used as his computer password. Plus, you were the one who gave Aldo the check he used in the forgery. I just put it all together."

[Chapter Twenty-One]

When The Chameleon did not get a response from his chief contact in Brazil, he knew that things had gone sour. He had to move quickly or agents would soon be knocking on his door, ready to escort him to jail.

He grabbed a large tote bag. It was the one that matched his shoes that were adorned with the heads of cane toads. He unzipped the bag.

The Chameleon held it up, stared for a moment, and then threw it down with a snort. He couldn't carry something like that around. He went to his closet and chose a plain black duffel bag. He found a pair of plain black boots stashed in a corner. Now he had to work out a disguise.

The Chameleon was angry and frustrated, but he wasn't worried. He had been in difficult situations like this before. All he had to do was go undercover for a while. Then he could start all over again.

He smiled to himself. Federal agents had been looking for him for years. He wasn't going to be brought down by some kids.

[Chapter Twenty-Two]

With the password he had gotten from Cody, Captain Montez searched Santos's computer. He found the information and the evidence he needed to crack the animal-trafficking operation wide open.

He didn't waste any time. Captain Montez moved fast, calling agents all over the world. They arranged for raids on warehouses at 9:00 a.m. the following day.

That was a lot of phone calls. They paid off. At 9:00 a.m. the next morning, police raided every one of The Chameleon's locations. The long arm of the law reached into many airports and captured an impressive number of smugglers.

While the raids were going on, one of The Chameleon's most trusted smugglers walked into an airport carrying a suitcase. He posed as a computer salesman based in Hong Kong who regularly traveled between that country and the United States. His name was Ron Carter.

Mr. Carter knew all of the customs agents. One was being paid off by The Chameleon to wave him through. His flights were always arranged to land when that agent was working. For two years, everything had gone smoothly.

That day Mr. Carter entered the airport as usual. When he approached Customs, he looked around for his agent. He wasn't there. Someone else was in his place and waving him over.

Carter didn't like the look of things. Still, he had no choice but to do as he was told. He only hoped that this agent, too, had been paid off. He took a deep breath and headed over to the agent.

Usually he'd be waved on with "have a nice day." Not this time. Instead the agent said something he dreaded hearing. "Please unzip the suitcase."

Ron Carter knew he was busted. He unzipped the suitcase and watched as the agent stared at a dozen sock balls.

"What have you got in there?" the agent asked.

"Turtles."

"Clay turtles? Wooden turtles?"

"No . . . real turtles."

The agent unwrapped the socks and found a dozen rare Arakan turtles from Myanmar. They were a critically endangered species once thought to be extinct. He shook his head as he took Ron Carter into custody.

Similar busts were taking place all over the world—in Hong Kong, Paris, Los Angeles, and other cities. In Singapore, a woman waiting in an airport departure lounge began acting strangely. First she began to squirm in her seat. Then she began touching her hair again and again.

The woman was wearing her hair in a large bun on top of her head. As other horrified passengers looked on, they heard a shrieking sound coming from inside the bun. Then it began to jump and twist. The woman began shrieking, jumping, and twisting, too.

Her hairdo began to unravel. Then a baby monkey jumped out and began running down the aisle as onlookers stared in shock.

Officials caught the monkey . . . and the woman. The baby monkey had been sedated but woke up earlier than expected.

When Otis heard about it through Captain Montez, he couldn't help laughing. "That woman sure had a *bad hair day*," he said, digging his brother in the ribs with an elbow. Cody just rolled his eyes.

But the high point of the entire bust was catching

The Chameleon himself. He was traveling in Europe when the raids took place. Amazingly, he was totally unaware of what was going on.

In New York's LaGuardia Airport, agents were ready and waiting for him. He was coming in from Italy, landing at 10:00 a.m.

Officials had been shown several pictures of the man. They were shocked by how different he could appear from one photo to the next.

One picture showed him as slightly plump, with short blond hair and blue eyes. In another photo he was darkly tanned with cold gray eyes and a greasy gray pony tail. In a third photo he was taller, with pale skin and black hair. He even looked younger than in the other pictures. But in a fourth photo he looked older, with a long white beard. They knew they had to keep a sharp eye out for this man, or they'd miss him.

They nearly *did* miss him. They'd been on the lookout for a passenger on Flight 151. They didn't know that The Chameleon always changed his flight arrangements at least twice, and always at the last minute.

The agents waited . . . and waited . . . and waited. There were quite a few, stationed along checkpoints all over the airport. Someone would spot their target, wouldn't they?

They almost didn't. Who would expect an international smuggler worth millions of dollars to be dressed as an ordinary businessman?

The Chameleon walked right past ten agents. He was wearing a plain gray business suit. He even waved at one of the agents. He thought he was smarter than everyone else.

As he got nearer the doorway, he began to walk faster. He was sure he had done it again. He enjoyed outsmarting the airport agents.

But then a tall, broad-shouldered man with a brown mustache stepped in front of him. He took The Chameleon completely by surprise.

"Excuse me, sir, I need to see your passport," the officer said.

Surprised as he was, The Chameleon didn't show it. He smiled at the officer. "Of course," he said. He began to reach into his pocket. Then he ran.

The Chameleon sprinted for the doorway, sending people scattering out of his way. He pushed past people who were wheeling their luggage or using hand trucks. He knocked people down.

Then The Chameleon spotted a moving platform that sped people along toward the exit. He jumped on it and began elbowing people out of the way.

"Everybody stand aside," yelled the agent who

had first spotted The Chameleon. He had already called for backup. Agents had radioed ahead and others were blocking all the doors.

Soon six other agents were racing down the moving platform after The Chameleon. But he was fast! And he was determined, too. He had never been caught before, and he didn't intend for this to be the first time.

But his luck had run out. As he jumped off the platform, two agents stepped in front of him, blocking his way. Then the one who had spotted him stopped him from turning around. Agents swarmed in from everywhere, and he was surrounded. He was only twenty feet from the doorway.

The Chameleon didn't give up easily. He hadn't gotten to be the biggest, wealthiest animal smuggler in the world by caving in.

When the agents of the U.S. Fish and Wildlife Service sat him down in an office and questioned him, he pretended not to know what they were talking about. He claimed to be an honest businessman on a holiday.

"The warehouses you are telling me about are breeding farms. I am exporting animals bred and raised in captivity. They are not wild animals."

"Nice try," said Sam Snell, senior agent. "We

have an old friend of yours ready to testify that you smuggled wild animals. You hired people to grab them right where they live. Sometimes you even hired poachers to pose as tourists to go to other countries to transport them."

A sleazy, self-satisfied smile spread across The Chameleon's face. "I can guarantee that none of my people would tell you that."

Agent Snell's next words wiped the smile off The Chameleon's face. "What about your old pal Aldo? He had plenty to say when we caught him red-handed. He sang like a canary when he wanted to help save his own skin."

Snell clicked his teeth with his tongue. "It's too bad you didn't try exporting canaries. Now there's a nice legal business. But that probably wouldn't suit you, would it?" he said as he leaned toward The Chameleon.

"You know, I've been in this line of work a long time. I'm tired of seeing guys like you who think they can get away with whatever they want to. Rules don't apply to them. Aldo was like that, too. Then they find out that they can get caught just like anybody else."

"I don't believe he said anything against me." The Chameleon laughed nervously. "Besides, what could he say? I run breeding farms."

Snell snorted again. "Any time you want to quit

lying, just feel free. Please make it soon because I'm tired of fooling around. I'd like to get home to my wife and kids by dinnertime."

But Snell didn't get home before dinner. He was lucky that he made it in time for a late-night snack. The Chameleon didn't give up easily. He kept saying that what he was doing was perfectly legal.

Finally Agent Snell made a call to Captain Montez in Manaus. He told him that he had arrested The Chameleon—Waldo Lou. Then he told The Chameleon what he had learned from Captain Montez.

The police had taken the computers and found e-mails between him and Aldo about trapping animals. They had e-mails about customers who wanted wild animals, too. And they had orders and invoices.

The Chameleon never confessed. But Waldo Lou knew that with all the evidence against him, they had him. And it made him really, really mad. But what made him even madder was hearing Snell tell him that his whole operation had been brought down by three 12-year-olds.

[Chapter Twenty-Three]

Maxim rustled the newspaper and sighed. "Can a leopard change his spots? Can a chameleon change his ways?"

"Not if you're talking about *The* Chameleon, Waldo Lou," said Otis. He was reading the same newspaper online. "At least the case against him is getting attention."

"Yeah, we've all been asked for our autograph at least once," said Rae. "It's like we're movie stars."

"Yeah, it's kind of awesome," said Cody. He was reading the newspaper online, too. "It says that Waldo Lou will go to prison for three years and pay a fine of five hundred thousand dollars."

"I'm glad things will work out for Pino," Otis said after a moment. "He'll have to do some public service as a penalty for getting involved in animal trafficking.

It's a good thing the judge took his age and the circumstances into account."

"Right," said Cody. "Pino seemed pretty eager to do the public service, too. I think he's really sorry for what he did. He learned his lesson."

"But then Mr. Estevez will let him go to Amazonas College of Art. I think he learned some lessons himself."

"Well, I'm glad that Pino didn't go to jail. But Waldo Lou's penalty doesn't seem to be enough to me," said Rae. "He did awful things and made plenty of money from doing them."

They were gathered in the Carson home, in the den. Their parrot, Pauly, a legally bred parrot that they had bought at a friend's pet shop, was sitting quietly on his perch. He was looking down at the family dog, Dude, a Labrador who was dozing on the floor. As usual, he was waiting for a chance to tease the dog.

Mr. Carson was standing in front of his easel in the far corner of the room. He was checking his progress on his latest painting. It was a picture of some monkeys playing in a tree. He had made the sketch for the painting on a trip into the rain forest that he made after The Chameleon was arrested.

He stepped back from the canvas. "No, it's not enough, but it's a start," he said. "Years ago he would have gotten off more easily. Animal smuggling is being taken more and more seriously. Waldo Lou was the biggest smuggler in the world, but there are other big ones still out there."

"That's right." Otis nodded as he peered at the newspaper on his computer screen. "That's because it's such big business."

"Illegal traffic in animals is estimated to bring smugglers about twenty billion dollars every year," Cody said.

"It's because people buy them," said Rae.

"It's true." Otis turned away from his computer. "From what I've read, it's kind of a cult. People want an animal that's bigger, faster, meaner, or rarer. But that's not the only thing that causes the problem."

"Yeah," said Cody. "These smugglers pay poor people to catch the animals for them. They need the money for their families."

"Some people need the money, but some just want it. Like the customs agents that take bribes to look the other way."

Maxim cleared his throat. "However, a lot of very good agents have been doing an excellent job of finding these smugglers." He turned a page. "It's a good thing, too. These people have no shame. The things they do are shocking."

Maxim went on to tell them about some of the recent cases. Many involved the smuggling of birds. "Illegal trafficking of all kinds of parrots has been busy," he said. "It's horrible. Birds have been smuggled in toothpaste tubes, hair curlers, stockings, and thermos bottles. They aren't fed and they aren't given any water."

He had to stop reading for a moment. "It's really terrible," he said.

"I know," Rae said. "We learned about it in school. Those birds are very fragile. More than half die just from the shock of being captured. And others die while they are being transported. They aren't given food and water, like you said, Maxim. And their wings are clipped to prevent them from flying if they get loose."

Cody joined in the discussion. "Yeah, it seems like they keep finding out things that are worse and worse. Smugglers know that about seventy-five percent of animals will probably die between being captured and transported. So they make sure to capture four times the number they plan to sell!"

"I read that a pink macaw from the Amazon rain forest can bring as much as a million dollars," said Otis. "We didn't see any of those."

"And listen to this," said Rae. "They just seized orangutans in Thailand. They were being forced to box for entertainment."

"Disgusting," said Maxim.

"At least we know that people are being caught, and animals are being saved," said Otis.

"Sometimes there's a funny side to it, too," said Cody. "Listen to this: a guy tried to smuggle in eighteen baby parrots in pouches that he had strapped to his legs. The customs agents wouldn't have caught him if they hadn't seen bird droppings splattered all over his shoes!"

Everyone chuckled. "He was in *deep doo-doo*," said Otis.

"*Har-har, rah-rah*," Cody smiled.

"Fetch! Fetch!" Pauly shrieked suddenly. He shifted on his perch, waiting for Dude to jump up.

But today Dude was too smart for him . . . or too lazy. He simply rolled over.

Pauly hung his head with disappointment. All of his feathers seemed to wilt.

"Attaboy, Dude!" Rae said. "Don't let that bird fool you."

"Let's get back to talking about those endangered animals," said Otis. "I want to do something for them."

"I think we should," Cody agreed.

"We could start a club at school to help endangered animals," said Rae. "Maybe we could have bake sales every month and send some money to the World Wildlife Federation or another organization that helps endangered animals."

"That's a great idea, Rae," said Mr. Carson.

"I know what we could do," said Cody. "We could make the baked goods in the shape of animals or decorated like animals. Imagine—panda cakes and toucan cookies, bear brownies . . ."

"Let's make some animal cookies right now," Rae said as she got to her feet. "It'll be fun."

"Uh-huh." Otis smiled. *"More fun than a barrel of monkeys."*

"You know, I never thought I'd say this," Maxim said, peering over his newspaper, "but these mysteries we've been involved in are actually pretty exciting. I'm beginning to look forward to running into another."

Rae, Cody, and Otis were speechless—but not for long. "We love them!" Rae blurted out.

"Yeah," Cody agreed.

"And you're right—we never thought we'd hear you say that, Maxim."

"Neither did I," said Mr. Carson. He stepped back and studied his painting. "I'm warming up to the mysteries myself." He glanced at Cody, Otis, and Rae. "You three seem to find them wherever we go. Let's see what happens on our next trip."